CLICK BAIT

CLICK BAIT

Gillian Philip

Copyright © Gillian Philip.

This edition published in 2019 by BLKDOG Publishing.

No part of this publication may be reproduced, stored in a retrieval system, or transmitted in any form or by any means, electronic, mechanical, photocopying, recording, or otherwise, without written permission of the publisher.

This is a work of fiction. Names, characters, businesses, places, events, locales, and incidents are either the products of the author's imagination or used in a fictitious manner. Any resemblance to actual persons, living or dead, or actual events is purely coincidental.

All rights reserved including the right of reproduction in whole or in part in any form. The moral right of the author has been asserted.

www.blkdogpublishing.com

My thanks for putting up with stupid questions, and providing useful and knowledgable answers, go to:

Richard Cantwell and everyone at Elgin Sheriff Court; Peter Milne of Elgin Police; Kenny Farquharson for patiently explaining the weird world of journalists; Fiona Dunbar, Lee Weatherly and Inbali Iserles for being fabulous critical readers; Ailsa Nicol and Sharon Black; and legal tweeters Malcolm Cameron and the mysterious Geoff Shadbold. You were all awesome and all the mistakes and potential offence caused are mine alone.

1 3

2 7

3 21

4 37

5 45

6 53

7 65

8 71

9 79

10 87

11 95

12 103

13 109

14 117

15	127
16	137
17	141
18	147
19	154
20	159
21	171
22	177
23	187
24	195
25	205
26	211
27	215
28	227
29	231

Nobody in Langburn, least of all Brodie Cumnock, would have believed someone would set out one day to kill him and his seventeen-year-old daughter in cold blood. These things didn't happen in Langburn, or if they did, they'd have the decency to happen on a slow news day when the town might at least have a shot at nationwide notoriety. Langburn did not have a lot going for it otherwise.

This is the sort of thought that goes through your head when you're sitting in a shed full of agrichemicals, crying and trying not to smoke, cradling a broken shotgun in your arms like a loathsome baby and wondering how it ever got this far. (Literally broken it wasn't. A broken shotgun is a safe shotgun. Then you snap it back together and it isn't. Broken means safe, as it so rarely does in other areas of life.)

This is the way you think. This is the way your head reels around, crashing into random notions like a drunk. But I'm getting ahead of myself. It's probably the fumes.

I'd better start at the beginning.

And I'd better finish at the end.

THE LAST THING THAT WENT THROUGH JOANNA RICKS' HEAD

What's on your mind?

Tempting little question. And when you've done something so wrong, so bad, so unforgivably loathsome that an entire trainfull of human beings is willing to throw you out of it rather than share it with you, there's kind of a big answer.

You go back and think about the whole sequence of events, over and over again, and try to work out the points where the parallel universes broke away and in those lovely unreachable worlds you didn't take the fatal steps. You imagine a universe in which nobody on that train even knew who you were, much less wanted to grab you and slam you against the door and then chuck you through it. You imagine a world where you didn't give in to the lure of a social media site, a world where you didn't *Write something...* And then you imagine an existence where you didn't click *Post.*

Rewriting your brain's history at three in the morning doesn't help at all. But you do it anyway.

So, for instance, if my car had been in working order, I wouldn't have been on that particular train in the first place. So I wouldn't have been there to get thrown off it; but I'm leaping much too far ahead.

I can trace it further back, just a couple of days. If the disc drive on my Xbox hadn't been irreparably damaged (which it wouldn't have been, had the kid next door not broken his Playstation and come round to have a go of mine), I'd have been peaceably shooting the crap out of Colombian drug dealers, or maybe hit-and-running a prostitute. Instead, I was bored enough to go trawling the internet for jokes.

"You ought to read a book," my old nan Flo would have told me, had she still been alive. And she'd have been right.

The joke itself, the one I found, was unimpressive, though I was impressed enough at the time to sort of half-choke, half-cackle at the enormity of it. Oh, let's be honest, at two in the morning and with a bellyful of vodka, Red Bull and Heineken, it was hilarious. If I hadn't thought so, I wouldn't have posted it on my own Facebook page.

Yes, I know it's sad and provincial but I still have a Facebook page. Or I did have, because I had Friends then, both with and without a capital letter, and if we wanted to get together, that was how we arranged it. Or we'd post photos of the resulting get-together: at least, the ones appropriate for any casually-stalking parents or uncles or grandmothers.

Occasionally, one of my eighty-odd Friends would share a stupid photo or a quiz or a joke. And before you have a go at me, I know I'm not the only one who hadn't updated my privacy settings since umpteen-sixteen.

If I'm going to explain myself, it would obviously help if I can explain the joke.

In the best tradition of sick jokes it started as a response to a major international tragedy, in this case 9/11. And the only person it was mocking, really, was the guy who flew one of the planes. I mean, it was tasteless, but it wasn't *victim-mockingly* tasteless.

So: "What was the last thing that went through Mohammed Atta's head?"

And the answer is:

(Wait for it)

"The tail fin of a 747."

I promise you, there's a surprising number of variations on this. If I'd posted the joke as was, it wouldn't have raised an eyebrow (though it was unlikely to have raised a laugh, either). The mistake I made was Adjusting For Topicality.

So if I tell you that six days earlier there was a blaze in a chemical storage facility in Glassford, resulting in an explosion and the death of a local, young, female police officer with two small children, you'll get the gist. So yes, I *did* amend the joke for local flavour, replacing the 747 with a barrel of chemicals. And before you ask: yes, I *did* post my drunkenly ill-judged joke on Facebook on the very eve of the woman's funeral.

That's the fickle irony of technology, then. If Xboxes were built to withstand a kick from a frustrated ten-year old, I'd never have turned into an involuntary YouTube star.

Gillian Philip

HOW DID I GET HERE (1)

So here's what happened, in case you've never seen the piss-poor phone footage. Of course you will have seen it; everyone did. You can't see my face very well, though everyone I knew knew it was me (and later, so did everyone in the country, and a respectable percentage of the world). And I understood, actually. In other circumstances it might have been me who manhandled me off the train and dumped me on the platform with a bloody nose.

Up till that moment, the Facebook thing had been localised (a bit like my joke). I woke up in the morning with a pounding head, a guilty conscience, and a Friends' list that was eight down. This didn't bother me, despite the clenching feeling of unease in my belly, since I'd never liked any of them, even at school, and I had no idea why I'd added them in the first place. There was a snotty little message in my Inbox from Aoife Connor, demanding that for the sake of human decency I take the joke down off my Wall, so I didn't. I posted a mildly amusing status about my hangover level ('Hedgehog'), and went back to bed.

I woke up again four hours later to an even worse headache (as you do), and a shitstorm. A localised shitstorm, but an intense one, like a frontal summer depression in the Cairngorm valley. There were more messages in my Inbox, which I read, swore at and deleted.

I did not, however, delete the joke.

I did that after a late lunch, when I had a bacon roll in my stomach and a text from Sid that said, 'Are you all right, you total tosser?'

Since Sid was right about most things, even in a coded fashion, I deleted the bloody joke.

At one point that afternoon I turned on the local news, whose main story was of course the funeral, 3pm at St Matthews, Family Flowers Only, Donations in Lieu to Glassford Police Welfare Fund. I'm not sure how well the Fund did out of this, because nobody took any notice: the cortege route was lined with silent crowds chucking bouquets at the hearse. When it reached the cemetery, two small children got out of it, each gripping the hand of a grim-faced red-eyed man in a black suit. The littler kid looked bewildered, the other was biting his lip and not quite stopping his tears.

The reporter barely had time to open her mouth before I switched off the TV. I switched off because that nasty little knot in my gut yanked down on my stomach, and I had to go to the bathroom and throw up the bacon roll and the remnants of the Heineken.

Click Bait

I didn't turn the TV back on till my stomach was empty and the afternoon schedule was safely ten minutes into *Murder, She Wrote*.

I needed fresh air and fresh groceries, so at about five I tried and failed to start my old wreck of a Vauxhall, then gave it up with a solid kick and a curse. I was going to have to forego Tesco own-brand potato waffles, but there was always the corner shop.

It was closed when I arrived, so I nearly kicked it too – the door, at least – but I heard the key turn and Mrs Slater opened it just as I was turning away. She looked a little startled at the sight of me, but she stood back and let me in, finding something fascinating to look at on my shoulder.

She was not her cheery self. She didn't even ask about my cat, and she *always* asked after Marvin. She *loved* Marvin. But she said not a word, and as she shoved my milk and rolls and bacon into a flimsy bag (and charged me a 10p bag tax without asking), she was a bit red about the eyelids. I know this because she caught my eyes at last and gave me a dead stare.

My hand had started to shake, so I wrapped the plastic bag handles tightly round my fingers.

"You were closed," I ventured pointlessly, for something to say.

She looked past me at the weather beyond the door: grey with intermittent sunspots.

"I was at the funeral," she said. "I was outside the church."

I had a good look at my numb whitening fingers while I waited for my credit card to clear.

"'S a tragedy," I mumbled, meaning it.

"Yes." She almost threw my credit card slip at me, like she was still in carnations-on-a-hearse mode. Her voice shook. "Those poor babies."

I could feel a hot tide of blood creeping up my face, so I nodded and slunk out.

Mad. Mad to imagine she knew. I doubted Mrs Slater was even on Facebook, and she certainly wasn't on my Friends list.

Still.

By the time I was sitting on the train into town, glaring out of the window and avoiding eye contact with my fellow passengers, I was feeling shakily relieved that I'd deleted that joke. By the time we pulled into Glassford station, I'd almost convinced myself that I'd posted a joke about Mohammed Atta on a plane, and never really had replaced him with PC Joanna Ricks (28), mother of Toby (8) and Calum (6).

Three hours into my shift, I was feeling positively optimistic. The bar was full all night and nobody spat at me, and nobody avoided getting me to serve them. Who's more popular than a barman behind a crowded counter? I was positively surrounded by smiles and waves and needy grins. Adrian the manager still liked me, using me loudly as a role model for the bone-idle Megan, who never seemed to do anything but moan about customers and her chipped nail polish. Even Brodie Cumnock, who owned the place, gave me a tight little smile when he came in to lord it with his partners. He thanked me, in his gruff way, when I carried a tray of drinks to his group in the special raised alcove. He even rolled his eyes, in mild amusement, at my cheesy grin and my lame attempts to suck up.

If I hadn't been so desperate to be liked that particular night, I wouldn't have stayed on a little too late to help clear up; so I wouldn't have been running for the very last train to Langburn.

It might not have saved me, in the end, but I wouldn't have been on *that* train.

How I wish that little sod next door had never kicked his Playstation.

*

That's exactly what I was thinking (or, ironically, what was 'going through my head') as I sat on a sodden platform with blood and rain trickling down my chin, very intently not looking at the train windows because I thought I was going to die of humiliation if I did. It took an age for the thing to hiss and spit and pull slowly away, and I swear to God the driver was taking his time so the guy with the iPhone could get a better picture.

Red lights dwindled smoothly away round the long curve of the track, and I was on my own. The silence when it was gone was beautiful and horrible. Well, until the sky exploded and started to rain nine-inch nails on the glass roof.

"Jesus," I muttered.

I didn't expect a reply. I slouched out, avoiding eye contact with the sniggering hi-vis staff. They must have thought I was fare-dodging. They'd know better in twenty-four hours.

Drew fecking Hunter. Drew My-Dad's-A-Police-Hero Hunter. Why did he have to be on that train, pissed up and *very* pissed off?

I'd seen him when I got on. I'd pretended I didn't. I'd picked up a discarded newspaper and held it in front of my face, pretending I understood Sudoku.

"OY. That's him. That's the cop hating c–_"

It wasn't just the word he used that got every single person in that carriage turning to look. There's a kind of voice that drowns out every other sound in the vicinity, and he was using it. The only thing to do in this situation is pretend you're deaf. I snapped the paper higher and stared at the pencilled-in crossword.

Eleven down. Legal turf (4,3)
"Eddie DOOLAN."

I wished this train would just get going. He must have gone to the pub straight from the funeral. I ran my eye down to the scribbled solution.

Sod's Law

Oh ha, ha. Thank you, Universe.

A stranger down the passageway was getting to his feet, and the guard was approaching from the opposite direction. I thought for a minute I was going to get away with it. Because the stranger and the guard actually were coming to my rescue, I reckon, before Drew Hunter got calm and steely and started talking rationally. And pulled a sheet of paper out of his jacket.

I knew what it was without having to see it; I really did. A screenshot. Aoife Connor took a *screenshot*.

I didn't listen. In some part of my mind I must have thought no-one would notice me if I sat very still. All I heard were angry voices and gasps of horror and a piece of paper rustling its way from seat to seat round the carriage. I just kept looking at the paper: *Sod's Law. Sod's Law. Sod's*—

When Drew grabbed me by the collar I started taking things seriously, but he had a good three inches on me, and the whole carriage was cheering him on by this time. For the sake of testosterone I put up a fight, but there was only ever going to be one outcome.

So there I was, in the middle of the night, wet and bloody and full of unjustified hatred. There was a rip in my jeans where I'd hit the platform, and for the moment that annoyed me more than anything. Heading for the exit, not looking at anyone, I lit up under the excuse for a shelter just outside the station entrance. Fourteen miles to Langburn, and it would be five in the morning before I got home. I might as well set off, especially since an officer of the law was approaching me with a fixed-penalty spot-fine gleaming in his eye. Never mind the spot-fine; right now the last person I wanted to meet was a member of the grieving Glassford constabulary.

I turned up my collar and half-sprinted down the road; there was no point him chasing me, since the rain extinguished my fag instantly.

"Eddie. Eddie Doolan!"

Not another one. I nearly didn't stop, because the way my evening was going I reckoned it couldn't be anything good. Still, I was drenched already, and my curiosity got the better of me. I stopped and squinted through forty-five-degree sheets of rain.

The passenger side window of the white BMW coupe was open, which couldn't have been doing its cream leather upholstery any good, but the girl driver was leaning across and waving one hand while she kerb-crawled me. "Did you miss your train?" she yelled.

If I didn't answer for a long moment, it wasn't because I thought it was a stupid question. I was surprised, was all. I dropped my sodden and barely-smoked fag onto the streaming pavement and stamped on it, unnecessarily, for something to do.

"Eddie! I can give you a lift back to Langburn."

I should have leaped at the chance, instead of standing there like a stunned ape, the rain trickling so far down my collar it had reached my butt crack. But all I could say was, "Where did you get *that*?"

"I stole it," said Lily Cumnock, with a beatific smile.

"Liar," I told her, before I could edit myself.

She shrugged. "I told you I passed my test! On Monday, remember?"

That was Lily's World: you pass your driving test, you have a brand-new Beamer three days later. This was a girl who already had one dressage horse, and a matching one on her Christmas list. Giving up any pretence at pride, I clunked the door open and got in. I was dripping all over the new cream leather, but Lily gave no sign of minding.

"You miss your train? Stay in the pub too late?"

"Yeah. *Working*," I said, miffed. "It's a job, Lily. Remember those?"

"Sorry. Didn't Adrian let you away in time? I'll tell Dad to have a word."

"Don't! Wasn't like that," I said in mild panic. "I didn't miss my train."

And I found myself telling Lily about what had happened on the train. Just the basics, obviously; I was tired. But it felt so raw in my chest I had to spit it out or I'd be eaten away from the inside; it certainly burned my throat on the way out.

I was furious: with myself and Drew Hunter and his mates and everybody else on the train who had watched and giggled and cheered. I was even mad at poor dead Joanna Ricks.

Lily let me tell the whole story before she said a word. When I ran out of words I sat silent, still fuming.

"But what did you *do*? I mean, *why* did they throw you off?"

I licked my lips. I licked them again. I cleared my throat.

"I posted a joke on Facebook. It was a bit sick."

"Naughty," she said, and slapped my thigh lightly. I half-expected to shoot out through the roof like James Bond in an ejector seat.

"A joke about Joanna Ricks," I added.

"Wh—" She turned, eyes wide. "*Oh.* Oh, *Eddie.*"

"I *know*. All right?"

She didn't say anything for a bit, just tapped her polished fingernails on the steering wheel and looked awkward.

"Everybody makes mistakes," she said at last.

"Thanks," I said, though I knew Lily rarely did. "Been a bit of a git."

Of course I didn't know at that point what a YouTube hit I was going to be, but for the moment, it made me feel better. Lily was a straightforward sort of girl. I said I felt like a git, and she believed me.

The windscreen wipers were going full-speed, sloshing the torrent away. I'd had a busy night and I was knackered, and the hypnotic beat of them made my eyelids heavy. When I woke up with a start, my head was bouncing off Lily Cumnock's shoulder and we were nearly on the pavement. There was my house in its little cul-de-sac on the very outskirts of Langburn, a couple of miles and a thousand light years from Lily's country pile further up the road.

"You're home," she said brightly.

"Oh. Right."

I put my hand reluctantly on the door handle, but just as I hoped she would, she slipped a cool hand round the back of my neck and turned me back towards her. I was more than content to be pulled around. For a girl who had never officially had a boyfriend—as far as her father was concerned, anyway—Lily could snog like a gold-medal Olympic snogger. The scent of her dark hair filled my nostrils and I could feel its silkiness against my face. I shuddered, and felt her smile against my mouth.

Far too soon she drew away and kissed my nose and stroked my freckles with her thumb and smiled and nuzzled my neck.

"Your dad would have an aneurysm," I reminded her, a little breathlessly.

"It's not *you*," she said defensively. "I told you. It's the schoolwork thing. The exam thing."

"Yeah."

"It's all right for you. You're finished with all that." There was a sulky turn to her mouth.

"I know, Lily. It's all right for me. I had the benefit of a Glassford Academy education, and you've got to struggle at that bog-standard Dunstane."

"Don't be chippy." She wrinkled her perfect nose. "I didn't choose it."

I sighed. "Sorry."

"You are forgiven." She put on her magnanimous face, which made me giggle. "Text me later, 'kay?"

"I'll call."

"Don't call. Dad'll hear it. Text, I said."

I did my Angry Controlling Boyfriend face, which made *her* giggle.

"Okay," I said. "Set your phone to vibrate and keep it in your pocket. He *definitely* won't hear."

She spluttered a laugh, along with a two-word epithet that would have got her expelled from Dunstane College.

"I only wish you would," I told her with a martyred air.

"My daddy warned me about boys like you." She leaned across me—which did *not* help—and shoved open the car door.

"Night, Lily," I said mournfully, still resisting.

She glanced at her watch, and bit her lip, and pushed me so hard I nearly fell out sideways.

"Good*night*, Eddie. Sleep well."

*

I didn't. The trouble with pub work is enforced sobriety, and the trouble with sobriety is that you don't get a few hours' grace. You don't lie stunned into unconsciousness for five hours till thirst wakes you up. And I knew I was going to feel even worse in the morning, so I didn't especially want to sleep. After I'd lain staring at the ceiling for an hour, my head buzzing and whirring with angry guilt, I threw the duvet and the cat aside, and got up to switch on the ancient laptop.

As soon as I could afford to, I planned to replace that machine, because it was old even before Flo died. It was achingly slow and there was stuff stuck between the keys that I didn't want to think about. Flo used to clean it out with Rizla papers, and they came out all brown. Still, the laptop did the job. Too well, as I was about to discover; but at that hour all was quiet.

Plenty of people were awake to chat, so long as they lived in the States. I saw the messaging icon blip into life with a request from Sid—and what was she doing up at this hour? —but I ignored her. Instead I half-watched YouTube videos and browsed Instagram and Snapchat, thinking about anything except trains and bad jokes, until I couldn't ignore the acrid tang of cat piss.

I swung my chair round to stare at Marv. He lay there on the crumpled duvet where I'd dumped him, stretching a paw affectionately towards me as if he'd like to touch my hand but couldn't be arsed. Around him on the polycotton pooled a growing stain of darker blue.

I picked him up, floppy and damp as a dead thing, and took him downstairs. When I opened the back door and dropped him to the ground he arched his back, then wandered idly into the bushes, but I knew he wouldn't want to stay out so I sat on the concrete step and lit a cigarette.

The half-moon was a scribble of white light behind the clouds. I leaned back on my elbows and blew whorls of smoke at it, wondering when I'd give up. I really had to, and soon. Lily didn't like the taste of it on my mouth.

I shouldn't have thought of Lily again, not at this hour, not when I couldn't sleep anyway. I crossed my legs, uncrossed them, pressed my thighs together. Heat rose in my cheekbones and I was glad I was outdoors in the cooler air.

Marv reappeared, writhing against my legs, so I stroked his back and tried to forget about Lily. Things were easy for young Marvin. Marv had lost his balls six years ago, and the rest of his mojo last year when he was hit a glancing blow by a motorbike. Now he didn't even dump dead mice in my bed. His incontinence seemed a small thing to put up with in the circumstances. Not that Flo had ever agreed, but then Marv didn't like her much either.

"You want to come back in?" I asked him.

He looked at me. *Stupid question.*

I ground my fag into a tub of half-dead begonias and lifted the cat into my arms. He smelt more of grass and warm skin than of pee this time, so I gave him a kiss on the back of his furry neck.

The sky was full of stars, the garden was scented with orange blossom, and even the bypass beyond the trees was more or less silent. Marv's purr was rumbling right through my skin and muscles, dissipating the desperate lust for Lily's body. There are just moments when you know it's a perfect calm before a perfect storm, but you've got to enjoy them when you get them.

Gillian Philip

3

Have you seen this video? Is this you?!!

We've all had those messages. And you're like, *Oh for God's sake, you've been hacked, and when will you learn,* and you delete the message and send back a snarky one to the idiot who was so unforgivably careless with their password.

This time, I got that sick plummet in my guts. My finger hovered over the delete button. Then the link. Then the delete button again. And then I thought, *I'll just have a quick look and I won't give anybody my password,* and I hit the link.

Oh.

Christ.

On. A. Bike.

I shoved back my chair from Flo's dressing table, and the cat fell off my lap with an indignant grunt. I couldn't swallow but nor could I take my eyes off the screen. There it was, in murky shades of scum: sixty seconds-worth of me getting what was coming to me.

So: Drew Hunter rips the newspaper out of my hands to display my face for the camera.

Me: *Look, I don't want a fight.*

Drew: Unintelligible snarl, including *Jo Ricks* and *little kids* and *feckin' ashamed of yourself. What have you got to say?*

Me: *Why would I apologise to you—*

Him: *You need to apologise to this whole town, you wanker. Jo Ricks was one of us.*

Me: *What are you, her mother?*

Him (to train): *Did you hear him? Did you?* Him (to me): *You're not even sorry, you piece of shit.*

Me: *Listen, you excuse-for-one, if I happened to be sorry, it would be fuck all to do with—*

And at this point some tattooed tosser shoulders in front of the camera and jams his face close to mine and says *I think you need to get off this train, son.*

This is the moment when I'm thinking the guard might come to my rescue, but though she's not on film, as I remember it she's got her arms folded and she's got a *don't-look-at-me-pal* expression on her face.

So there's a bit of a silent stand-off, ripe with the scent of righteousness. That lasts two seconds on the little bar at the bottom, while somebody behind the iPhone jolts its owner's arm as he rises for a better look.

And *then,* just as I'm opening my mouth either to apologise and calm things down, or to swear mightily at the pair of them and throw a punch—to this day I'm not sure which I'd have chosen—Drew Hunter hauls me out of my seat and wrenches my arm behind my back, and Tattooed Tosser's got me by the neck, and between them they're wrestling me to the door, except it's just shutting and my nose crashes into the glass.

And then you can't make out exactly what happens: just a melee and some shouting and Drew's shoving me again, and shouting *That's for Jo Ricks*, and then we disappear, and then the two local heroes are back in view and I'm not, and the carriage is erupting in cheers.

Replay? suggests YouTube sweetly.

*

I had to take a lot of breaths—not deep ones, because I couldn't—before I could bear to look at the hit counter.

30,000. And rising.

I pushed the laptop away and put my head on the lovely cool desk till I stopped thinking I was going to throw up. Marv padded across the scattered papers, and whacked my head out of sheer spite, but I barely felt it.

Look on the bright side, I told myself. *You're a git, Doolan, but you can hardly see your face in that video. Nobody outside of this godforsaken town is going to know it's you.*

And then I checked the comment thread.

*

I knew a few of the names commenting, and they certainly knew me. What I hadn't previously known was exactly what they thought of me, but I suspect in a few cases they hadn't actually thought it till that moment. All the same, it was a bit hurtful to see my old Geography teacher on there.

I had some experience with comment threads, but not really from this angle. It felt surprisingly personal, even when it was coming from a total stranger in Vancouver. (*Vancouver?* Of course, they were still awake in Vancouver. It wasn't six in the morning there.)

YouTube? How was a Canadian finding his way to an obscure bit of Scottish iPhone footage?

I knew the answer before I even opened my Tweetdeck. In fact as soon as I thought the word 'Twitter', my stomach fell into my lower intestine. And it didn't take long to find the hashtag: #WhatWentThroughEddiesHead.

I added a dedicated column for it, because obviously I wasn't feeling bad enough. And it wasn't the sharing of the YouTube video that bothered me most. It wasn't even the accompanying comments. It was when I spotted Aoife Connor's screenshot flashing past.

Sonofa*bitch*. Sharing it around Langburn and Glassford wasn't enough, then. Aoife and Drew had felt the righteous urge to go global. And had it ever. I was trending in the UK.

I had to put my hand over my mouth, or all the Rizla papers in the world wouldn't have been enough to clean out the keyboard. I kicked back the chair so fast it tumbled over, and bolted to the bathroom.

I clutched the bowl for a while, breathing hard. *Fifteen-minute wonder,* I told myself. *It'll be over by five o'clock tonight. Calm down.*

So I did. I took big breaths and flushed the toilet and staggered to my feet. I crept back to Flo's room on tiptoe because, you know, if I moved cautiously enough, Twitter might forget I was there. Very delicately I picked up the chair and set it silently back in front of the laptop. I eased into it without breathing, and clicked the mouse slowly and silently to get rid of the kitten screensaver. I swallowed, blinked hard, and leaned in to look at the screen.

Which was the exact moment Danny Kingdom retweeted the screenshot.

*

Danny Kingdom. Never liked him, never liked his chat show, hated his diabolical comedy road movies, never found anyone who would even admit to liking him. Which didn't stop him having 3.2 million followers. His famously dimpled face smirked out at me in a thousand retweets, or that was what it felt like as the column speed went turbocharged. His words were illegible for about ten hours (or again, that was what it felt like), but at last I managed to read them.

Wondered what the fuss was, but look what #WhatWentThroughEddiesHead he tweeted sternly, but with an endearing twinkle. *Amazin what people will do for a bit of attention. If ever a twat deserved to trend its this twat right here. Still laughing Eddie? Twitterstorm long range forecast: this one -like Eddie's gob- will run and run*

He'd had to work at it a bit to keep it to 280 characters plus screenshot: you could tell from the placement of the dashes and the bad punctuation. I concentrated on that detail for a *long* time. After that, I slightly adjusted my new fantasy of throttling Drew Hunter with a chain, and imagined doing it to Danny Kingdom. Now *that* would get me in the headlines.

In the world of Twitter I was news: I was racing up the charts, and not in a boyband way. My hashtag went from ninth to number 1 trending topic in a matter of minutes; in the natural way of things, Danny Kingdom was followed by a few celebrity friends of his own, and when they retweeted it in turn, it became too ridiculous to be real. A cold sensation flooded through me from my scalp to my toes and all the way back up, which was fine, because otherwise I might have been sick again. Instead I felt numb. Lots of people didn't have the words for how they felt about me, but they certainly had the emojis. The little dog-turd one was a favourite. Enraged tweets were coming in from all quarters now: Germany, Dubai, California, Hong Kong. If there were any nice ones, they must have got trampled in the crush.

I shut down Tweetdeck. Then, just to be sure, I switched off the laptop altogether, staring at the screen till it blipped to black with its usual painful groan. Watching that laptop hibernate was like watching an elderly relative go to sleep; I never knew if it would come back to life again. This time, I'd have been glad if it didn't.

Flo's room was in darkness, the faded flowery curtains still shut. I made myself go in there regularly, just to prove to myself that I could, and besides, it felt like a burrow where the world couldn't go. The film of dust on the dressing table had thickened, so you could no longer see the square where the laptop used to sit.

I sat down on the single bed. It still smelt of her: Victoria Beckham scent (yes, I know), Scholl cracked-heel cream and gin. The gin was fading.

I lay back and stared at the ceiling. The soggy springs were giving me a backache already but I was too tired to care. That raggedy stain was still on the ceiling; I decided it might have got bigger, and I hoped it wasn't dry rot. There were dirty stains on the wall too, beside the headboard. If I got some paint I could smarten that up. It might take five or six hours to paint the whole room. I could clear her stuff out, too. Take the old clothes to Oxfam. It would kill a whole day.

Then I'd just have all the other days to get through.

I shut my eyes so I could ignore the stains. The silence in the room was very soothing, really. I could just stay here. Forever and ever and—

My phone buzzed against my groin, then burst into some racket of a ringtone I didn't remember choosing. I got such a shock I bounced off the bed, which hurt my back again, but I didn't manage to fumble it out of my pocket before it switched to voicemail. I think maybe I'd fallen asleep.

After I'd sat staring at the phone for a while, I decided it was unlikely a stranger could have got my mobile number, so I tapped the screen nervously and listened to the voicemail. Sure enough, it was Sid. The late Sid. The way, way too late Sid.

"I wouldn't look at Twitter if I was you," said the Voice of Doom. "Actually, don't go online. Anyway, want to go to a movie?"

I shoved the phone back in my pocket. *As if.*

I flopped back onto the lumpy duvet and eyed the ceiling stains again. Several deep breaths later, I felt calmer. This was not Twitter. This was my house and it sat in a cul-de-sac on the edge of my home town, which happened to be in the sweaty armpit of nowhere in the eyes of any Californian tweeter or pissy actor-comedian. *This is Real Life*, I reminded myself. *I'm not online. I don't need to open that laptop again. Ever. It's not as if I ever liked it.*

I thought I'd better start the day, since I was due at the pub for a lunchtime shift, so I unhooked a dressing gown from the back of the door and shrugged it on. I opened the bedroom door just fine, but for some reason it took me a lot of deep breaths before I psyched myself up to walk downstairs. My heart was palpitating in what seemed like a most un-masculine way.

In the kitchen I was greeted as always by Flo's little Jesus action figure on the sideboard, its jointed arm pointing right at me. Mysteriously, its face looked exactly like Gerard Butler. The batteries had run out ages ago, and he had stopped beckoning me rhythmically towards salvation. The sideboard he stood on didn't fit the room anyway, and I cracked my hipbone on it as I walked past. *Like always.*

I had to get rid of Flo's stuff, I really did. Next week I'd get down to it. I mean, she'd been dead six months.

I was boiling the kettle and frying bacon when I heard the usual rattle on the window. I rolled my eyes and slouched over to open it.

"Can I use your Xbox," said Crow.

I stared at him. Scrawny, bad teeth, *and* suffering from short-term memory loss.

"It's not fixed yet," I said. "Since that time you broke it."

"Oh. Can I come in."

"No."

He screwed the toe of his trainer into the dead grass. "Just for a minute."

"You're meant to phrase that like a question. Like, 'Just for a minute?'"

"Just for a *minute?*"

"No."

He sniffed the air like a scrapyard terrier. "Is that bacon."

The little bastard had never heard of question marks. "Yes, and it's burning."

"I won't eat any then."

I sighed and unsnibbed the back door. Crow slunk inside, and Marv wove between his legs and went out. I made Crow a bacon sandwich and he took it.

"You'll want to know about—That's different, by the way." He eyed Flo's old quilted floral dressing gown, frayed at the sleeves, the one she called a housecoat because she went to Canada on holiday once.

"It's warm and it's useful and I sleep in the nuddy," I snapped. "You tell a feckin' soul and I'll disembowel you. What will I want to know?"

"Somebody decorated the front of your house."

"Why couldn't they decorate the in—oh, *shit*." I marched through to the hall and opened the front door. And shut it again, just missing the camera flash.

Back in the kitchen, Crow watched me sympathetically. "I was going to warn you about the reporters, but you didn't wait."

"Who *are* they?" I sat down and rubbed my hands across my head. The one bite I'd managed of my own bacon sandwich wasn't going to stay down. "How did they know?"

He shrugged. "Well there was reporters up for the funeral anyway and the polis tipped them off because they knew about it by then because Drew told his dad like straight after it happened and his dad told his mates. So there was that. And the man out there, like, he's a local guy, he lives in Glassford and he's a stringer whatever that is, and he does stories for the big papers and he's got mates in the polis, but anyway the big head editors and that at the papers, they told him to look into it, like, cos they saw you were trending on Twitter and he doesn't do Twitter but they told him. And he's got a photographer guy with him with a camera."

"I *noticed*. And there's just one of him, right?" I could hardly breathe because my heart was galloping out of my ribcage, but Crow had paused for breath and I had to get in there when I could.

"Yeah there's just him, well him and the photographer guy, but I told you, like, he's a *stringer* and he works for the big papers and he's doing the story for a few of them like, so it's going to be in the papers tomorrow and anyway it's going to be on the internet before then. Like now."

"So what," I said through my teeth, "is he doing. Out there. If he's got his story?"

"He's wanting an exclusive interview. Like for one of the papers. Because like the story's going to be all over the place after tomorrow and it's not just his story anymore. So there'll be like more reporters all over it he thinks. So he's wanting an exclusive. Cos he can like sell that. He gets more for that."

The little bastard finally ran out of breath. His scrawny chest was rising and falling almost as fast as mine.

I unclenched my jaws, then ground them together again. The reporter had found me so fast. Faster than a speeding Tweetdeck column. And Crow knew so much about him.

"Did they have sweets, by any chance?" I asked him savagely.

He nodded and pulled about nine packs of Haribo out of his pocket.

I rubbed the bridge of my nose between my thumb and finger. I shut my eyes and tried to think. "What's on the front of the house?"

"Dogshit. Mostly."

"Mostly," I echoed.

"Must've been a big dog and all." Crow grinned.

"It's all your fault," I said, pathetically.

"Right." He looked confused, justifiably. "You'd better go out the back."

*

I better had, but I got dressed first. If I was going to get my fifteen minutes of notoriety, I didn't want it to be in Flo's old housecoat.

Now that I knew they were there, I could hear the two guys outside, gabbing into their mobiles and occasionally swapping jokes (tasteful ones, presumably). So I elbow-crawled into my own room, excavated my clothes from the previous day and crawled back across the landing to Flo's, with its conveniently-shut curtains. I'd have liked to peek out and see the state of the front of the house, but I'd have had to open the window and lean right out, and no way was that happening.

I did manage to peel the curtains open a crack, just enough to see the impressive new paint job on my car. Oh well, it's not like it was working anyway. At least they'd shelled out for nice yellow gloss paint.

TROLL FILTH RIP JO

Jesus Gerard Butler, it was like having Flo right there with me again. I could almost hear her online voice.

Her poor kids didn't deserve that bless them & bless their lovely mother, rest in peace Jo.

OK, Flo, I didn't mean it and I wish I hadn't done it.

You should never have a moment's rest. Its the good that die young when evil creatures like you are free to post there filthy hate. Your free to grow old and miserable and I hope your happy. When you need a policeman I hope there not around for you because Jo will never be around for her kids.

I know, Flo. Your right. (And now you've got me at it.)

Crow had got bored and disappeared with a few of my newer DVDs, so at least I could have a few moments' peace in the kitchen while I summoned up the nerve to open the back door. When I finally managed it, I nearly fell over Marv on his way in, but there was nothing human in sight.

The watery sun was warm enough to bring out the bees in the tatty back garden and make the path smell of cement dust. Clearly the gods had had enough of tormenting me for the moment, and now they were sitting back with their feet up and their hands behind their heads, taking bets on what I'd do next. I was wondering that myself. I was too early for work. All I knew was that I couldn't stay under siege in Flo's bedroom, with her ghost whispering in my ear.

What the hell. I slung my jacket over my shoulder, yanked open the gate and made a rapid walk for it.

They came out of nowhere, the two of them, one brandishing his camera. Out of instinct more than quick thinking, I swung my jacket down and shoved my arms into it, but naturally I got one arm caught and had to fight with it to get it on properly, and only then could I turn up the collar.

Waves of heat surged through my body as I tried to push past.

No such luck.

"Mr Doolan? Eddie Doolan! Jack Michie. How does it feel to be a viral internet hit, Mr Doolan?"

I understood with sudden blazing clarity why people punched photographers, but I was just of sound enough mind not to do it.

"Mr Doolan! Have you got any comment? Do you have anything to say to Joanna Ricks's family?"

I racked my dead brain.

"Would you like to apologise now, Eddie?"

Yes, I know. What I *should* have done was stop and look long and soulfully into the camera, and tell the slavering world I regretted my actions very much and it was a spur-of-the-moment piece of ass-hattery and I didn't ever think it would go this far. And I promised never to do it again. And I'd have my back, sack and crack waxed for Comic Relief, if that's what it took.

I didn't say any of that. The heat in my skin was so horrible it was actually going to make me sick, waves and waves of panic and shame pulsing through my brain, which never makes it easy to think. All I could do was keep walking faster and faster, while they tailed me down the road at a brisk jog.

Michie shouted after me. He wasn't in the flower of his youth and he was out of breath. "Are you aware of the Communications Act 2003, Mr Doolan? Section 127! Do you know you've committed a criminal offence?"

That made me almost trip over my own feet, because the fact was, nothing of the sort had occurred to me. I gave a noncommittal grunt of surprise, which sounded not in the least apologetic. It just sounded like a grunt. A good yobbish one. The camera clicked like silenced gunfire behind me.

"The police are saying—" he began again.

"EDDIIIIEEEEEE!"

I halted, wobbling in surprise, and looked up from the pavement. A skinny arm was waving at me wildly from an open ground floor window, and the wave turned into a frantic summons, and the window was hoisted wide with a violent crash.

I didn't even think. I did a smart military left-turn into the weed-ridden yard, marched straight to the window and swung first one leg, then the other, over the sill. It was really quite a stylish move, except for the bit where I got tangled in the blowing net curtains. I shoved them out of my face and jumped down, and Sid slammed the window shut behind me.

I was breathing hard. I was roasting hot, too. I stripped off my jacket while she flung the curtains shut with a flourish.

"Thanks, Sid."

She put her hands on her scrawny hips and tilted her head to examine me. "You are *such* a twat," she said.

"Okay. Well, if that's all you wanted to say I'll be—"

"Never occurred to you it might be a slow news day, did it?"

"In Langburn?" I growled. "Always is."

"Everywhere. You were on the six o'clock news. Or your Facebook page was."

I stared at her, dumbfounded. That wasn't fair. Social media was social media. The news was what my middle-aged boss watched.

"Have a cup of tea. And then you can go out the back door."

"That's working well so far." I flicked a resentful glance at the street. "And I'd rather have a Coke. With ice."

Sidonie Stewart was a world champion at visual sarcasm. It was one of the ways she got by at school; nobody wanted to be on the end of one of her Looks, like I was now. You'd have thought she'd be easy meat, but it's amazing what an unfaltering Evil Eye can do. Most of the bullies were superstitious enough to be scared of her: and her an acne-ridden, lank-haired nerd with a mouth full of metal and a body that made Posh Spice look overfed. Whoever said you can never be too rich or too thin, it struck me, had never met either Lily Cumnock or Sidonie Stewart.

She looked at me long enough to make me blush with embarrassment about treating her like a waitress, and then she gave in and got me a Coke. Something like a Coke, anyway: I think it was Lidl own-value-brand, by the taste of it. But it was cold, and she'd slung in some ice cubes.

She frowned quizzically. "Is that broken?"

I touched my nose delicately. "No. Just a mess."

"It looks quite good actually. A face can be a bit too perfect."

Sid had a way of taking me aback. "Well, cheers."

"It's true, is all. Maybe you should punch Lily Cumnock while you're in the mood."

I was more inclined to punch Sid. "That's a bit bitchy."

"It's a bit true. And how's it bitchy? I'm just saying you're both pretty."

"Honestly, Sid—"

"You see? Looking like this means I can say what I like. Mind you, not that *you* have a problem opening your gob and sticking both size twelves in it. Obviously."

Sid gave me such a huge and infectious grin, I laughed instead of getting mad.

"See?" she said. "You feel better already. Let's go out. You and me."

"You mean, er…"

"Oh just *go out*. On a one-off basis. You have time to kill and I'm bored. Not that you shouldn't go out with me, like *go out with me*. You'd have much more fun with me than you have with Barbie."

I ignored that, with its ring of truth. "So, do what?"

"Hunter-gathering," said Sid, and smiled her metal smile.

4

This was why it was out of the question for me to go out with Sid in a romantic context. At some point, her wacko parents would have invited me back for dinner.

I was regretting even the generic cola drink by the time Sid reappeared from the depths of a filthy cupboard, clutching a khaki backpack that smelt stalely of butcher-shop. I caught myself licking my teeth and wondering if the Stewarts had a private water supply, and if so, how they made their ice.

Sid's grandfather was a keeper. I don't mean that once you had him you'd never let him go: I mean he was a gamekeeper. He lost his job and his tied house twenty years ago and moved to the town, but the Stewarts still lived in an episode of The Archers from 1952. That included Sid, though the closest she'd come to country life was a Saturday job in the fruit & veg department at Morrisons Langburn.

And hunter-gathering, of course.

Sid and I picked our steps through assorted dirty boots and unlatched the back door, then clambered up through what Sid called the Rockery (because it was a pile of rocks with some weeds in between) and escaped through the splintered back gate. The woods were lovely, dark and deep; and if you watched your feet you wouldn't get Alsatian-shit on your Converse.

Avoiding the drifts of last autumn's beech leaves, we headed for the bare-earth track that would take us down to the B-road that joined up, in about half a mile, with the main Langburn-to-Glassford road. I was only going to walk Sid as far as that, then wait for the bus. I did not care if I had to stand in the shelter chain-smoking for an hour and a half, I was *not* pulling a sickie and going home for tea with Sid. Even though she asked me to, as soon as we were over the fence.

Really, she was remorseless. Also, shameless. It would have been a lot simpler having a crush on Sid, but the heart is never that convenient. I was stuck with Lily till she moved away to a high-powered job in London and I had a chance to get over her. And Sid was not an option.

She swung the smelly backpack at her side as we trudged along the dirt path, then chucked it at me as she climbed over the sagging wire fence. I caught it before I realised what I was doing, and flinched.

"Bad luck about Drew being on the train," she said as I followed her over the fence.

"No kidding." I threw the backpack at her. At least we hadn't hunter-gathered anything yet, but I wiped my palms on my jeans anyway.

"You'll be a while living that one down. There's stuff on my Snapchat like you wouldn't believe. I bet you're glad you've left school."

"Yeah, but I've still got to live in this town."

"Got to live anywhere in the country, judging by that news report. Ah, here we go. That's a good start."

A good start was the headless badger on the verge, though on closer inspection it had been there a bit too long. We stood over it, watching the flies breed.

"You wouldn't eat a badger anyway," I said.

She didn't answer, so I didn't push it. I didn't really want to know for sure. I didn't know if she had entirely rejected Mr Badger, so I set off down the road and hoped she'd follow me. Sure enough, I heard the slap-slap of her feet on the tarmac as she ran to catch up. Sid wasn't an elegant runner but I reckon she could lope along for hours, like an orc.

When I came to a standstill, she nearly ran into me. I pointed. "How about that?"

Sid gave a little squeal of pleasure and crouched to lift the pheasant by a wing. Its crop had burst when the car hit it, and raw grain was spilt across the tarmac like a serving suggestion. I watched her stuff the bird into the backpack; one claw stuck out of the flap, pathetically, as she slung it over her shoulder and grinned at me. Weak white sun sparked off her braces and I caught myself wondering what they'd feel like against my tongue.

"Does any of this actually taste nice, or are you just being cheap?" I asked her, in a sudden bad mood.

"You don't know what you're missing," she leered in a clear double-entendre. "Speaking of which, have you seen Barbie since the…er…?"

"Yeah. But that was before it was in the news. I might have edited things a bit."

"She'll be all right. I'm sure she won't dump you. More's the pity." She wrinkled her nose. "Oh look!"

I was pleased to be off the subject of Lily; less so when I spotted the distraction. It was not much more than a dark obstruction on the road when we spotted it, but as we came closer I could see the antlers.

"I am *not* trying to get that into your bag," I said. "See you later."

Sid had come to a halt; she looked almost tearful. "It's alive."

"All the more reason."

"We have to do something."

I was afraid she was going to say that. "We can hardly hit it with a stick."

The deer was sitting on the road with its legs tucked underneath it, for all the world as if it was just having a lie-down. I thought maybe it hadn't seen us, but as we walked carefully around it, its big black doleful eye followed us, rightly suspicious.

"Broken a leg," she said. "In shock. We have to get a gun."

"You got a gun? Because I haven't. Not since that high school massacre." I stepped back as a motorbike veered round us, wobbling before it raced on.

"Ha ha." Sid frowned. "I'd have to go all the way back to the house and get Dad's, and it might've crawled off by then. Or caused a crash. How hard could you hit it if we found a big stone?"

"Not hard enough." I shuddered. "Let's just leave it." A car slowed, then swerved past, the driver throwing us a filthy look. "Wasn't *us*," I yelled pointlessly after it.

"Better phone somebody. A vet?" She had the Sid Stubborn look.

Sighing, I took out my phone and googled *Langburn Vet*. There was one practice, and two bigger ones in Glassford. Sid was pacing round the deer, far too thoughtfully for my liking. "You won't get it in the bag," I reminded her. "Hello?"

They could have somebody out there in an hour, said the voice on the phone, so I repeated the timescale to Sid. She shook her head, scowling.

"The Glassford vets'll take even longer," I pointed out as I dialled.

"Well, try them. Oh!"

The deer clearly distrusted Sid's stalking behaviour as much as I did, because in a sudden panic it scrambled to its forelegs and dragged itself frantically towards the grass verge, eyes rolling and mouth frothing. Maybe it had only just realised what had happened. Its hindlegs followed it, drawing a broad line of dark blood on the tarmac.

"Shit." Sid scampered after it, while I let the phone hang at my side, half-hoping the deer would indeed crawl away and take the responsibility off me.

Its not a person its an animal. You shouldn't put people down like you put animals down, humen life is sacred, but that's not the problem here Eddie, its an animal and its better out of it's misery.

Flo was always right, even when I was imagining her.

Besides, the deer was not letting me off the hook. It had got only as far as the shallow ditch, where it crouched and quivered, like a kid hiding with its hands over its eyes. I felt terrible for it.

"Eddie, *do something!*"

I don't know if I felt sorrier for the deer or for Sid, but I found myself rummaging in the undergrowth for a big enough stick. I've no idea what I thought I could achieve, so thank God for the throaty roar of another car, one that braked this time. I stood up just as its shiny blue bonnet rocked to a halt in front of me.

"What a mess." Brodie Cumnock climbed out of the Mercedes and leaned on its roof to stare at the injured deer. The door on the other side swung open too, and Lily stood up.

God. The last people I wanted to see right now were my ultimate boss and my unofficial girlfriend, especially since Lily looked so uncomfortable. Brodie had never been mad keen on her going out with me, to put it mildly. I was pretty sure he didn't even know we were still a Thing. Still, she could barely catch my eye. I frowned.

"It wasn't us," I said, nodding at the deer.

"I never thought it was," said Brodie. "What are you going to do?"

"Have you got a gun?" asked Sid.

"It's in the boot."

Well, that was handy.

"I'm taking it for maintenance before the shooting season starts," he said, like he realised he needed an excuse. "After I drop Lily off."

Brodie opened the boot, unlocked the metal case that was welded into it, and took out the bits of gun. As he clicked them together, I glanced at my watch and shifted from foot to foot. At least Brodie could give my excuses to Adrian if I was late at the pub.

He slid cartridges into both barrels. "I'm not familiar with—Where's the best place—"

"Oh, give it to Eddie. He'll do it."

Thanks for that, Sid. I took the broken gun from Brodie and snapped it into working mode.

The deer was looking downright antsy now, its eye rolled back at me in an oh-no-you-don't expression. I couldn't think about this too long so I stepped up, snuggled the stock into my shoulder, pressed both barrels to the back of its skull and squeezed the trigger.

The explosion sent Lily about two feet in the air, though Sid didn't react. She folded her arms and watched with interest while the deer jerked and lunged and kicked.

"You didn't kill it," said Brodie in horror.

"Yes, he did." Sid rubbed its staring eyeball with a thumb. The kicking subsided at last and the deer's bloodied tongue lolled from its mouth.

"It didn't look instant." Brodie's face was oddly white. I suppose he'd only shot birds before.

"Well, it was. Eddie shot it in the back of the head, for fu—"

"Okay!" he interrupted. He couldn't take his eyes off the thing in the ditch.

I grabbed its antlers and pulled its head back to expose the shattered jaw. "Can I go now? I've got to get to work."

"Ah," said Brodie Cumnock. "About that."

5

I couldn't let it go. I should have, because I didn't have a moral leg to stand on, but what I did instead was simmer around town all day, avoiding anyone who looked vaguely like someone I might know. The sun had burned off a faint mist; the women had bared their scorched arms and shaded their infants' buggies, at least one fat man was eye-achingly topless, and the war memorial was crowded with bored teenagers making occasional forays into the pound shop. I might have known some of them, but since nobody shouted to me, I gratefully assumed that I didn't. The stares I felt burning into my shoulder blades must have been imaginary. Sharp as switchblades, but imaginary.

At four o'clock I headed for the bar.

It was a quiet time of day. The lunch crowd gone, the after-workers still to arrive. I knew Adrian would have no excuse for avoiding me. In retrospect, I wish he'd found one.

"Disgusting person," said Megan softly but clearly.

I pretended not to hear her. "Bye," I told Leanne without actually meeting her eyes.

Leanne ignored me, and turned on the hoover.

*

I always thought it was a stupid name anyway, The Whistling Frog. Brodie Cumnock had the idea on one of his annual Christmas jaunts to Barbados. The nightclub was called Green Lizard. The other pub, the one a few miles into the country with a play area and a beer garden, was the Cane Field Club. You ask me, he was showing off. But he certainly didn't leave much in the way of alternative workplaces.

I didn't have much choice but to go home, killing some time with the bus journey (I still wasn't going near the train). My pay-off wasn't going to last long, but I didn't want to sign on, didn't know if I even could till I got some kind of formal letter. I think I was still living in stupid hope. Megan was going to be absolutely crap at my job (combined with her own, if Adrian was telling the truth about downsizing) so I had a tiny nugget of hope that he'd want me back.

The tiny nugget popped and shrivelled as I turned into my own street. In the small-mercies department, Jack Michie and his photographer had given up for the day. But somebody had added to the dogshit-and-paint mural in broad daylight, and it struck me like a slap that none of the neighbours had tried to stop them. One of my downstairs windows looked odd and blank, and when I got a bit closer I realised somebody had put a brick through it. Where the hell was Sid when you needed her?

That question, at least, got an answer. There was a scraping sound and some shadow-movement round the side of the house, and in the early evening sunshine I saw Sid appear like an ugly angel, dragging the garden hose. She saw me, and stopped. Light gleamed off her braces, but her smile was a bit half-hearted.

"I thought you'd be working," she said.

"So did I." I hesitated. "Not any more."

"Oh. Oh, shit, Eddie. So he was really serious? Was it Adrian that fired you?"

"He was the front man. Brodie Cumnock did the kicking."

Water was trickling feebly out of the end of the hose; the water pressure never was any use. Sid stuck her thumb over the end of it and tried to spray the front door, but it wasn't having much effect. She kept blinking, and I think she just wanted to avoid looking at me.

"It's not much use, is it?" I said.

"S'pose not." Her hand fell to her side, and the water started to soak her trainers.

"But thanks," I added. "I think I want to go inside now."

"Yeah. The Hills Have Eyes, don't they?" She gave me a sudden grin.

"Yep." I glanced at number 44, and saw a curtain fall back into place.

"I'll make you a coffee. C'mon."

At least it was out of my own tap this time. I unlocked the door, getting yellow paint on my fingers; Jack Michie's scribbled note on the doormat was the only thing handy for wiping it off. So when I got round to reading it, half of it was obscured by lurid yellow blotches.

> *sure you want t*
> *your side of thi*
> *ould love to get the story from your poi*
> *in your interes*
> *can be assured I'll put forward y*
> *ublic sympathy*
> *f you're trying to find a way to mak*
> *apology, we can make that a big part of th*

I crumpled the sticky paper and sat at the kitchen table, staring glumly at Jesus Gerard Butler, while Sid did unspeakable things to a mug of Nescafe. It was weak and she hadn't let the kettle boil properly, but I didn't feel like having a go at her.

She pulled out the chair opposite, and slumped down, clasping her hands behind her head.

"What about Lily?" she asked.

"Lily who?" I snapped.

"All right, all right."

"He didn't like me going out with her before anyway."

I shouldn't keep checking my phone for a message from Lily. I shouldn't. But I did it anyway, about twice a minute. I knew I was only making myself sick. Lily did not have a rebel's heart. Not a heart-of-hearts, anyway. She'd liked the thrill of defiance in going out with me, but she was a nice girl and she loved her father. What I'd done was effectively prove him right about me, and I'd be amazed if I ever heard from her again.

That's what I told myself in my rational moments, anyway. Since my rational moments were few and very intermittent, my entire epidermis was on permanent alert for a phone vibration in my pocket.

I did feel sick now. I felt really sick. I pushed the coffee away.

"Brodie's never liked *anybody* going out with Princess Lily." Sid made a funny little face of disdain that almost made me laugh. "I took some flowers up to Flo."

My brain whirled about a hundred and eighty degrees, then settled in a foggy morass of offence and resentment. I hated that Sid had thought of it. I hated her, on the spot, for being a better person than me, and also for not being Lily. "Why'd you do that?"

She shrugged. "I figured you won't be going up to the cemetery any time soon."

To be honest, I hadn't thought of that. My lunchtime taco lurched up my throat. I wrestled it back into submission.

"Your nan was such a nice person," said Sid, picking at a loose bit of formica on the table. "She was very caring."

"She certainly was," I agreed, perhaps a little savagely. *Not like me, then.* "You're right, though. I shouldn't go up there for a bit."

"Best not to associate with her, er... her grave. For a bit. There's still a lot of people—you know. Going up to the—*other* grave."

"What did you take?" I wasn't that interested.

"Carnations."

"Flo couldn't stand carnations."

"Yeah, well. I didn't know that." She looked offended.

"It doesn't matter," I said. "It's not like she'll mind. She's a cadaver."

Her eyes softened. "Oh, Eddie."

I might have punched her then for the sympathy, except that the door bell rang. Flo had put in a fancy bell with a sweet little melody: the kind that makes you want to tear the face off whoever rings it. So what with that and Sid's sentimentality and the possibility of more reporters, when I flung open the door I probably wasn't wearing my best face.

Which was a pity, because it was the police.

6

Why didn't I chuck the laptop in the river while I had the chance? Pretty obvious why not, really, but that was what went through my head (and I have to stop using that expression) over and over that night. The two cops took me and my laptop down to the Langburn station, where they told me the court was letting them have the laptop and my phone as well. They had a warrant and everything. They arrested me and interviewed me; they swabbed my mouth for a DNA sample and took my fingerprints. Flo would have had conniptions. I don't know if they really expected answers, but all I did was mumble a lot and give an occasional grunt that could have been a yes or a no. I didn't know what to admit and I didn't know when to keep my mouth shut, so I mumbled. And grunted.

It wouldn't have helped if I had drowned the laptop. The police can find anything. They can get anything off a hard disk. And yes, it did occur to me to use the 'I was hacked by malicious persons unknown' line, but I knew fine it wouldn't fly. They didn't actually charge me, but there was nothing too positive to take from that; they'd be compiling a report and sending it to the Procurator Fiscal, they said, and he would take the decision about whether to prosecute.

Then they let me loose, and I had to walk back past what felt like every window in Langburn.

When I got home the alfresco press party had grown a little more, but I ignored their hopeful shouts and tried not to shove anyone as I wrestled my way through. I slammed the door behind me and locked it and put the chain on, and wondered if I should call a lawyer yet.

I still couldn't believe it was going to go that far, but I dug my old phone out of a drawer and plugged it in anyway. It was slow and it took forever to charge (God, I missed that laptop already), but I managed to discover that I'd probably qualify for Legal Aid, seeing as Brodie had made me so conveniently jobless and I had a bank account of minus-something, and that was before my latest credit card statement came in.

I tried to think of circumstances in which the Procurator Fiscal would recognise a joke when he saw one, and actually think it was quite funny, and hell, the lad was only nineteen, and boys will be boys, and what's the point in prosecuting him when he's *obviously very sorry indeed.*

I bookmarked the Legal Aid page.

It was odd, not having Flo's laptop in the house. I sort-of missed it, its physical presence, and I sort-of felt cleaner and lighter, as if the problem lay with a knackered old bit of hardware rather than intangible code that now floated loose in the world, off the leash and out of control, free to its thirty-thousand viewers.

Actually, make that nine hundred and eighty-four thousand, five hundred and twenty. (Twenty one. Twenty four. Thirty two. Sixty.) Because the old Sony phone worked perfectly fine when it was charged, so there was no escaping my own twattery, and no pretending I hadn't actually done what I'd done. Meanwhile on Twitter, a lot of people were mis-spelling the #WhatWentThroughEddiesHead hashtag, so I checked all the variations I could think of, and wished I hadn't.

I considered ditching the second phone, but that wasn't very practical. I had a job to find, after all. And of course I had to be there if Lily happened to call me. Not that she had, even after I'd texted her several times that morning.

I was getting used to the chronic sick feeling in my belly, which anyway was good for disguising the ache of no contact from Lily.

The doorbell tinkled its adorable tune, and my stomach lurched. I could make out shapes beyond the frosted side panels and I knew it was Michie again, so I backed down the hall and ducked into the lounge. Getting down on my knees, I crawled to the window, then lifted my head and peered over the sill.

There were a couple of new arrivals now and they all acted like long-lost pals, chatting among themselves. There was a sleek-haired woman with red lipstick, a grey blazer and a microphone: she gave a raucous dirty laugh when a guy with a goatee beard muttered something and scribbled on his notepad. Jack Michie was passing round the surplus Haribos; Crow must have sold himself too cheaply.

A man in a Led Zeppelin t-shirt was shifting his shoulder awkwardly under the weight of a TV camera. A TV camera.

A television. Camera.

Oh God God God God.

Jack Michie pressed the doorbell again. And once more with feeling.

There was only one place for me to retreat to and that was Flo's room, where the curtains were still shut. I tugged on her housecoat over my clothes, because it was chilly up there; it always was, because I hadn't turned on the heating in her room since she'd died. Or at least, I hadn't done it after the first time. There was a smell that I might have imagined, but it felt real to me, and whether it was in my mind or impregnated in the walls, I didn't trust it to have dissipated.

I lay down on her bed, in the dent she'd made over the years, and thumbed my phone, hunting for Flo's Facebook page. It still sat there onsite, more immovable than a granite tombstone. I had her password, and I could have deactivated her account, but it would have felt wrong. It would have felt like disrespect, and I didn't owe her any more of that.

If I'd wanted to find her last actual post, I'd have had to scroll down for miles. All the more recent messages were In Memoriam stuff, send-offs to a dead woman from friends she'd never met.

Still miss you, Flo. Rest in Peace xxx

(Richard White, Carrie Laws and 57 other people liked this.)

Too good for this world, sweetheart. Sleep well. <3

(Tony Higgs, Richard White and 34 other people liked this.)

Miss you Flo, miss your mischievous smile and your warm heart. RIP xx

(Mo Chambers, BernieLoves Dogs and 37 other people liked this.)

Somebody had posted a photo of a violently orange sunset, with a poem running through it in cursive script. A little shiver of distaste went down my spine when I saw that, but that was, of course, wrong of me; Flo would have loved its syrupy triteness. They meant it sincerely: that's what Flo would have said. She'd have appreciated it. And at least there weren't any sodding kittens.

Lots of people loved Flo. So it was true what she always said: it's the good ones that die. Except that Flo would Never Say Die. She'd say 'passed over', which to me always sounded a lot creepier.

Anyway, even the memorial postings had petered out after a couple of months. People do forget, whatever they say. Poor Flo.

She hadn't wanted to be forgotten, not ever.

*

The police had told me I'd get my laptop back, but they weren't saying when. I wasn't sure I wanted it back. And I dreaded what they'd find on it besides one dumb joke.

Summer has its disadvantages, and one of them is that it doesn't get dark enough soon enough. I had to sit on Flo's bed for hours, obsessively checking my phone, before dusk finally dulled the light and the flowery curtains turned opaque. I reckoned the reporters had gone to the pub long ago, but I still wasn't exposing myself to daylight. It was after midnight before it was dark enough for me to creep downstairs, wriggle out of Flo's housecoat and open the back door, then duck-and-scrabble my way round the front like a spy in a bad movie.

I'm sure the neighbours at number 44 weren't the only ones who watched me hosing and scrubbing at the dogshit (there was no shifting the yellow paint. I was going to have to paint the door and dump my car). I could feel eyes all over me like nettle rash, but I didn't turn, not once. I just hosed and brushed and tried not to inhale, and I focused on the headlines that were stuck appropriately in my head. Online headlines, of course, but I'd try to steer clear of the newsagents tomorrow.

They hadn't used the photo of me sticking my head out the door (Sid told me later that was only because they couldn't), so I was spared the sight of myself sporting the housecoat in a national daily's online edition, but there were plenty of shots of me walking away from the house with my jacket half over my face. Actually there was a little video of that. Even while I watched it, I wanted Eddie Doolan to turn round and punch the cameraman, but he didn't. Stupid Eddie just ran up Sid's path (did I really look like a girl when I ran?) and legged it over her open windowsill (not as graceful as I'd thought at the time). What with the reek of the dogshit, which I thought I would never get out of my nostrils, I was in a mood to concentrate very thoroughly on every single online comment that had stuck in my head, which was quite a lot of them. I think I thought that if I wallowed in them hard enough and long enough, I'd get over them faster.

Hope this guy never has kids.

Be funny if his mother died. (Wouldn't know if she did; haven't seen her for years.) *Preferably in a gas explosion.* (It wasn't gas that killed Joanna Ricks, it was chemicals. Get it right.)

The guy who chucked him off the train should get a knighthood.

Anybody who can laugh at two motherless children shouldn't be allowed kids himself. (You already did that one.)

Can only hope he gets cancer of the testicles, except he obviously hasn't got any. (Comment recommended by 234 people at the last count; replies included a lot of 'LOL!'s and 'PMSL!'s and crying-with-laughter emojis.)

You're all giving this git what he wants, attention. Best ignored.

I loved that commenter. I would have loved to be Best Ignored, but there was no sign of that happening any time soon.

I unrolled some black bin bags, ripped them and sellotaped them over the hole where my front window used to be. It wasn't much use and the tape didn't stick well, but it would have to do for now; I had no desire to expose myself to the neighbours again, so to speak. When I'd done what I could about the front of the house, I went round to the back of it. Marv hadn't shown up for his supper and I was pretty sure he'd turn up soon—not being the kind of cat who actually likes the outdoor life—so I reckoned I'd have a smoke and wait for him.

By the time I'd crushed out the first tab-end, I was worried.

I stood up and dusted off my jeans. I shouted, "Marv."

I don't know what he'd been doing: hiding and shivering till he got up the courage, maybe, because on my third shout he came out of the scraggy azaleas like a rocket. I hadn't seen him move that fast since the motorbike taught him to fly. He shot between my legs and I had to stagger back and fling open the back door before he could brain himself on the catflap.

"Marv," I said, following him in and slamming the door—because he'd creeped me out—"what happened?"

I picked him up and cradled him. He was shivering and there was blood on his nose, and he was purring like a steam engine, but not because he was happy.

"Did you get in a fight, furball?" I wrapped him up in his favourite towel and took him through to the lounge so that I could sit on the sofa and cuddle him. After a few minutes, he fell asleep, still purring, but in a different tone. I knew he was asleep because my lap was suddenly warm and wet, and I smelt of cat piss.

I couldn't be bothered moving. Jeans could always go in the washer anyway. And I didn't want to disturb him. Marv would never voluntarily get in a fight, so I reckoned he'd been set upon by the feline equivalent of Drew Hunter, and I felt extreme solidarity.

So when the doorbell started again early the following morning, and I opened it—because I'd slept on a sofa under an incontinent cat and I was only half-awake—I smelled like a litter tray; but at least I wasn't wearing Flo's housecoat.

Jack Michie recoiled when he got a whiff of me, but give him his due, he recovered quite fast. He smiled at me.

"At six a.m., Jack?" I said.

He looked flattered that I'd remembered his name. "Hi, Eddie. Can we come in?"

I looked at the photographer and I looked at Jack. The photographer was grinning at me, his camera gripped against his breast.

"What are you gonnae offer me?" I asked Michie. "Half a kilo of Haribo Tangfastic?"

He laughed. "He's a good kid, that Russell. No, we just want to chat to you, Eddie. Talk about it, you know? The Twitterstorm. The online stuff. The whole clusterfuck, yeah? Can't have been easy for you. Can we come in?"

"No." I was still catching up from realising who Russell the Good Kid was. Of course we only called him Crow because he hated his first name, which his mother had inflicted on him after watching *Gladiator* on Netflix. He's lucky she didn't call him Maximus.

"See, we want to tell your side of the story, Eddie. Show it from a different angle. Your angle."

"I'm not sure there is another angle," I said. "I think it's pretty linear."

"You're getting crucified, Eddie. Online, in the papers. Don't you want to at least explain yourself?"

It was Jack Michie whose lips were moving, but I was only hearing Aoife Connor's self-righteous whine. I shut the door in his face.

And then I went back to bed.

Well, Flo's bed. My own room smelt more strongly of dogshit, and however unpleasant the lingering odour in Flo's, it wasn't as bad as that. I couldn't smell much of it at all if I pulled the duvet over my head and curled in on myself, so that's what I did. I'd left the door slightly ajar, so after a while I felt Marv claw himself up the frilled valance, nearly pulling the duvet off me again. When he finally scaled the bed, he squirmed under the duvet and curled up against the hollow of my stomach. The vibration of his purr went right through my bones. We lay there in the darkness and tried not to think.

Well, I tried. Marv never did much thinking.

Flo would have been livid to find that cat in her bed. Under the duvet and leaking onto the sheet, no less. I'd always thought she'd appreciate a cat, being a single retired lady—and after all she loved photogenic kittens on Tumblr—but it turns out people aren't that predictable. When I brought home the flea-ridden kitten, she cooed obediently and touched its neck with the very tip of a painted fingernail, then swiftly retreated to wash her hands with Fairy Liquid. And that was the last voluntary contact she ever had with Marv. Knowing Flo, she was probably afraid she'd die alone one day and the cat would end up eating her.

Marv was deprived of that opportunity, but I really wish Flo hadn't died the way she did. She honestly didn't deserve it.

Flo had been an occupational therapist for thirty-five years by the time she retired, and she retired way too early. But she had to, she said. It was her knees, and her back, and the young guard rising up the ranks with postgraduate diplomas clutched in their ambitious fists. She was desperate to retire, so as soon as she could, she did. Maybe she thought her colleagues would keep in touch, and they did to begin with, but most of them were younger than she was and inevitably their calls and visits tailed off. If there's one thing an NHS employee is, it's a Useful Member of Society. And seeing as her colleagues still were Useful Members, they had better things to do than sit in her overheated front room drinking Flo's supermarket own-brand gin with orange squash.

Poor old Flo.

The thing about Flo was that she knew I was a good boy. She'd always thought so and nothing would ever make her stop thinking it. Indeed, she was always loudly on about it, in a sort of ongoing reinforcement programme. Flo never stopped believing she could turn me into her. Flo never stopped believing that one day I'd appreciate kitten gifs and sunset views and very bad rom-coms. And Flo never stopped believing that one day I'd find the right girl.

She told me so one evening, maybe two years ago. I'd come home to find her bustling round the kitchen—and my God, Flo did *bustle*—and I'd put my arms out automatically to catch her if she tripped and fell. Flo always looked to me as if she had the wrong centre of gravity. She was this chunky little thing, balancing too much bulk on the shoogly props of her surprisingly shapely legs. She still wore tight skirts, and big belts to throttle her waist into—well, something like an actual waist—and she was never without her makeup. I don't believe I ever saw her face naked. Except for that last time, of course.

"You should sit down," I'd said, whipping my arms back to my sides in case she noticed my over-protectiveness.

She'd turned her head and her fuchsia lips curved up at the sight of me. "I couldn't. I was too worried about you, sweetheart."

"Nothing to worry about," I said.

"You're late." A snappy couple of words, bitten out to camouflage her anxiety. But then, as if she realised she'd been too abrupt, she had fluttered her lashes at me, and I remember wondering if she'd put on her falsies. (Well, of course she had. What was left of Flo's eyelashes didn't flutter.)

"I was out," I said, "seeing Lily."

That was only partly true. I'd been out, and I'd seen Lily, but I hadn't actually dared ask her *out*-out, not that time. I'd seen her in passing, and we'd chatted, and then we'd sidled away from her girlfriends and we'd had an illicit few drinks together until her panicking friends tracked her down.

"Oh, Lily *Cumnock* Lily. She's a nice girl. She'd be lovely for you."

Privately I'd always thought so too, of course, but I didn't feel like admitting it right then.

"Lily's all right," I said grumpily.

"Don't let that father of hers tell her she's too good for you." Flo sniffed. "If anything it's the other way round."

Uh-huh.

"All the same, Eddie. You don't want to be sticking with the one girl. Not at your age."

Yes, I did.

"Oh, Eddie, love. Don't give me your Evil Eye. Come here, sweetheart, I missed you."

In a hug, Flo only just came up to my chest. All the same she could enfold me entirely, between her arms and her cloud of Victoria Beckham. I remember her big bangle digging into my kidneys, but I didn't want to let on. I just let her cuddle me, like a very oversized baby.

She pulled away at last, and I inhaled hard despite the Victoria Beckham.

"I kept your tea for you, love."

I'd had mine already. I'd had a kcbab with Lily. But I ate Flo's hamburgers anyway, because I really didn't want to upset her.

The last thing I ever wanted to do was upset Flo.

7

I wished people felt the same way about me. The columnist in the Daily Mail had no qualms whatsoever about my tender feelings. I felt I ought to read to the end, though, if only because she'd clearly taken so much time to think about me. In a parallel universe it would be flattering.

"You're kind of famous," Crow told me, through a mouthful of bacon roll.

I leaned back on my chair, tilting it onto its back legs, and gave him a filthy glare. My coffee was getting cold again. "You remember me asking you to get that bacon?"

"Mmph." He nodded.

"And what else did I ask you to get?"

His pale eyebrows shot up. He pointed at the roll, and chewed some more. "Owes."

"That's right. The rolls," I said. "What else did I give you money for?"

He looked dumbfounded. His forehead creased as his eyebrows dipped together. He chewed more slowly for a bit, and swallowed, and shook his head in perplexity, and finally said. "Nothing. You didn't ask for nothing else."

"That's right, Crow," I said through my teeth. "I didn't ask you to get me a sodding paper, did I?"

"You're reading it."

"Yes, Crow. Yes, I am."

"You're, like, you're getting a lot out of that paper."

"*Yes,*" I said, "There's a *lot* of reading in it."

"Well." He shrugged. "So."

I shook the paper out viciously and glowered at it. After a minute or so, I managed to start taking in the words again. Oh boy. Deborah Lake *really* didn't like me.

What I should not do was pull out my phone to read the online comment thread, so of course, that's what I did. It was an uncommon jewel among comment threads, in that almost everyone was in complete agreement both with the columnist and with each other. There was one isolated girl (I think) sticking up for me, but she was clearly of unsound mind, so I disregarded her opinion.

I closed the page on my phone. Flipped the paper back to pages four and five, which they'd dedicated entirely to me. I knew Crow was watching me, but I focused on the photos. I really did look like a shifty coward as I legged it down my own home street (thanks, Jack Michie's pal; I hope they paid you in Haribo); but those weren't the worst.

The worst was the gigantic picture at the top, spreading right across five columns: Joanna Ricks in jeans and pink jumper, laughing into the camera, each arm wrapped around an adorable young boy. The boys wore Minecraft t-shirts and cheeky grins. The smaller one's eyes were creased tight shut, because his grin was so massive. His older brother had a quieter smile, and his little arms clutched his mother ferociously. Joanna's long hair was blonde and her smile was white and her greeny-blue eyes were sparkling. Fixed on me, they sparkled with fiery hate. *You bastard, Eddie Doolan. How could you hurt my boys like that?*

The compare-and-contrast shot was taken at the funeral, and it only showed the boys from the back, thank God and the child protection rules. This time it was their father's arms that were round them; they were hunched into their smart jackets and their heads were bent forward. I was very glad I couldn't see their eyes.

There was a box of text in the bottom right: a bullet-pointed list of famous internet bullies and their victims. I read that bit, remembering some of them (I vaguely remembered being properly appalled at the third and the fifth, and recoiling in disgust from Number Eight). As for the actual story that took up all the space between the photos, I hadn't read past the first paragraph, which started: "A happy mother poses with her sons for a family snapshot. She was a brave and dedicated police officer whose sense of duty was as strong as her love for her little boys. But none of that mattered to vile internet troll Eddie Doolan…"

Which was as far as I could bear to get.

I threw the Mail with some feeling into the corner of the room, where it joined a growing pile of slightly smelly trash. Crow had brought me the *Sun* as well, but there wasn't much room for story in that, what with the enormous black letters that said **HERO COP'S TRAGIC TOTS**. I kicked it aside with my heel and picked up the local rag.

If there's one good thing about local rags, it's that they don't sully their hands with why-oh-why columns about the sociopathy of our nation's desensitised young men; I was in there, but only as a brief report, with that same unflattering picture by way of illustration. They were leaving the Moral High Ground to the nationals, and why not? The nationals were really amazingly good at it.

If I'd thought the *Glassford Examiner* was going to cheer me up, I was delusional, or maybe just desperate. I'd only just flicked past the usual happy seasonal photos down at Breakness beach—*School's Out: Glassford, Langburn and Breakness Bask In Summer Sun Fun!*—when a feature jumped out and slapped me hard in the face.

The Force Is With Local Businessman.

That was their sub-editor's lame way of saying that Local Businessman was actually one hundred and fifty percent with the Force.

Cumnock hands over cheque to launch Jo Ricks Foundation.

There was a photo, of course: Brodie wearing a solemn, intense smile as he handed a giant cheque to a senior policeman in a peaked cap and a lot of gold braid. I read the article underneath the picture, because it wasn't as if I'd made myself miserable enough. Brodie Cumnock might have been 'streamlining' some of his operations—by the way, I was yet to hear of anyone else who'd been 'streamlined' from the Whistling Frog or any of the others—but he could still afford to chuck several thousand pounds at Glassford Police Welfare to kickstart the new fund in memory of Joanna Ricks.

Not that he was all about the money, or not exclusively. Brodie could donate time and energy just as easily, which was why he and daughter Lily

(17) would be running the Glasgow Marathon in aid of said foundation.

In that moment I really, really hated Lily Cumnock. I hated her so much, I had a cigarette in celebration. No Glasgow Marathons for me, boys, not if I could ruin my lungs to help it.

"Can I have one of those," said Crow, startling me. I'd pretty much forgotten he was there. Round my place he'd always been an extra piece of unwanted furniture, like Flo's sideboard.

I peered at my cigarette and scowled. "No."

He shrugged. "They kill you anyway."

"That they do, Crow. That they do."

"You shouldn't smoke then should you."

My turn to shrug. "Don't see it makes any difference."

"You're stupid," he said.

"And you're barred." I stood up, nearly knocking my chair backwards. "Piss off, Crow. I've got things to do."

"My mum's not home." His mouth turned sulky and he glared at me.

"Is she ever? Not my fault," I snapped. Then I sighed, relenting. "Come back if you get hungry."

"Fine." He helped himself to a roll from the bag and stuffed it into his pocket. "Are you signing on."

"Probably. Go away."

Crow slouched out one way, and Marv slunk in the other. I was permanently under siege from broken things.

And reporters, but at least they weren't in the bloody house.

I couldn't just sit here. The police might be letting me simmer at a gentle rolling boil, but I couldn't afford to wait for their outcome, because my pay-off from the Whistling Frog hadn't been much more than I was already owed. And I really didn't want to sign on. I turned the *Examiner* awkwardly to Situations Vacant, trying not to read a single further headline. I folded it over. I started ripping out little squares of job description. When I had sixteen of them, I made myself a cup of tea, brought Marv to my lap for reassurance, and picked up my phone.

8

Danny Kingdom tweeted the family portrait. Of course he did. *The butt of #EddiesHead 'joke', guys. #RIP Let's remember Jo like this, and let's hope he's forgotten forever eh?*

Yeah Danny, *if bloody only.*

He gave the whole thing a nice kick forward on the internet, which kept the ball rolling and bumping along for the papers. I was up too early for Jack Michie and his pals; maybe now the story had been splashed all over the papers it was dying down? A faint hope fluttered under my ribcage, but in spite of Danny Kingdom's regal command, I doubted they'd forgotten me.

There was no sign of Crow and he'd eaten everything that was left in the house. I didn't go to Mrs Slater's for my groceries, and I was glad about that later; I pulled a baseball hat down over my eyes, swallowed to get my heart out of my throat, and ventured into town.

The Tesco Express was my safest bet for bread and milk and bacon. Unfortunately it also had a lovely big display of the daily papers, and I physically couldn't walk past those without glancing at the headlines. My throat was so tight I could hardly breathe, and my peripatetic heart had now climbed to the top of my ribcage to thunder just below my collarbone, but a wave of relief made me downright dizzy. I didn't feature on a single front page.

But I had to be sure. And because I'm a masochist that way, I bought a Star and a Mail and took them through the self-checkout.

After which I went round the side of the shop, leaned against their giant wheelie bin, and made the most terrifying phone call of my life.

*

I bet he'll say he was hacked hahahahahahahaha.

Just as well I decided not to take that line, then. I congratulated myself on my unusual foresight as I flicked foam off a strawberry frappe with my straw. There was a galaxy of drying pink spots all over the table, and I knew the barista was annoyed, but I wasn't meeting her glare. I kept my cap over my eyes and my stare firmly fixed on my phone, where at least I was in some control of the vitriol. I could turn it off, right? Although I didn't seem physically capable of doing that.

There were a few links on *#WhatWentThroughEddiesHead* that looked promising. I scrolled through the Tweetdeck column. Some left-wing hack was objecting to Internet Shaming, so I clicked through to his article.

Nobody with a working empathy gland thinks it was funny, he opined, right from the start. *Nobody could argue, as in this case* [hyperlinked to some other poor bastard], *that it was intended ironically, that it was a badly-phrased attempt at satire. But—*

I didn't get past the *but*. I was too preoccupied with the first unexpected churning of resentment in my belly. Tosser, making click-generated revenue off *my* nightmarish asshattery.

It wasn't that, though. It was his face on the byline avatar, and his knowing little smirk, and his folded arms.

No, it wasn't that either. It was—it was *I was drunk and it was late and I wasn't thinking and I DIDN'T FUCKING MEAN IT.*

I kept trying to read the article, but now that the anger was simmering nicely, I couldn't make out a word of it. It was nothing but dancing pixels. So I went back to Twitter, where I discovered via a couple of links that, as Danny Kingdom had revealed, the hashtag had been shortened to *#EddiesHead* to allow for fifteen extra characters of outrage in every tweet. You'd be amazed how much savagery you can add with fifteen characters: like caramel syrup on your latte. But I kept reading, because it was creating a delicious numbness in my guts. The numbness in turn was a nice blanket for the anger.

I was starting to decide not to be sorry.

The digital time display on my phone went from 11:31 to 11:32. *Two minutes late.* He wasn't coming. Of course he'd come. No he wouldn't. Yes he would. An entire panto audience was hollering in my brain.

My fingers felt swollen and clumsy as I unfolded the *Daily Mail* and turned the pages.

Oh.

I'd been demoted. That had to be a good thing, right? I was relegated to page 7. Still, there was new news.

"F#¢% YOU FOREVER AND I HOPE YOU DIE OF CANCER":
HORRIBLE HISTORY OF JO'S TROLL

Vile internet troll Eddie Doolan has a history of online abuse, it was revealed today...

Revealed by what sodding psychic? I thought of the smirking face of the police sergeant on the station desk, and I knew. The frappe tasted suddenly like engine oil.

The story was coupled with some of the more entertaining tweets from my hashtag (lazy bloody hacks), a few fresh photos of my victim (she was mine now, not a random chemical barrel's), and a compilation of character sketches from Glassford citizens who had once romanced me, shared playgroup Duplo with me, or taught me Geography. Hell, if I'd ever bought your bacon, cleared your dirty beer glasses or wiped your table, you got your quote in the *Daily Mail*.

Leanne the cleaner.

Megan the Dozy Barmaid. (Seriously? *I* was surly?)

Adrian Fairsworth.

Mrs Slater. ("I wouldn't have believed it of him": well, at least that was flattering, in a twisted way.)

My cousin Billie. (Bitch.)

Mr Morgan my Geography teacher. (Benefits of retirement. At least he used to slag me off in the privacy of the classroom.)

Caitlin Robertson. (I used to go out with her in Third Year.)

Click Bait

I had put my head in my hands before I remembered my baseball cap, and I accidentally shoved it right off my face. It tumbled to the floor. A huge fat guy at the next table did a double take and gripped his skinny latte tighter. His face reddened with righteous fury as he nudged his wife and muttered to her; then he half-turned to me and opened his wobbling mouth to say something.

Luckily, the door swung open at just that moment, admitting a cold gust, a woman with a pushchair, and Mackenzie Clark. All my fear and unrighteous fury dissolved in a pathetic surge of hope. *You came,* I thought; *you came, I knew you were my mate.*

I'd invited Mackenzie to a soulless coffee chain because nobody I knew went there (and also because it was one of the few places in town Brodie Cumnock didn't own). All the same I wished I had a fringe to hide under in lieu of my cap as I hunted needily for eye contact. Mackenzie did have a fringe, and he looked as if he was using it as a screen as he glanced furtively around the tables. I wiggled my fingers to catch his attention. Honestly. Wiggled my fingers.

His body kind of sagged as he noticed me, and I decided to interpret it as relief. I kicked out the chair opposite me, by way of a manly invitation. The fat bloke subsided into his own seat, muttering resentfully.

"Hey," said Mackenzie.

'Hey." I nodded. "You getting a coffee?"

He shook his head.

Okay, that wasn't good, because it meant he wasn't staying long. *But he came. He's my mate. He still is.* "How's it going then?'

"All right."

I was starting to regret the strawberry frappe now. It didn't look exactly businesslike. Or manly, for that matter. We sat in silence for a moment, as Mackenzie swung his foot against the table leg and drummed his fingers on the table. Abruptly, as if making a decision, he brightened.

"Well, you've been a bit of a dick," he said.

I nearly died of happiness. "Yeah," I grunted.

"Ach, it'll all blow over," he said. He was starting to look a bit more relaxed. "Everybody's a dick sometimes, right?"

"Right," I said.

"I mean, you deleted it when you were asked, I mean."

"Yeah," I lied.

"You're kind of famous now," he said.

"Yeah." Why did everybody have to say that? "In a bad way, but yeah."

He looked at his fingers. "So how's it going otherwise? Is that wee Crow still bugging the arse off you?"

Normal conversation: I wanted to kiss him. I wanted to kiss myself, just for having the idea and the nerve to ask him to meet me. For the next twenty minutes I had such a normal life, I almost thought it was permanent. Xbox Live. Football results. That girl at school who wouldn't go out with him but he thought she might change her mind now he had a job. That posh girl at another school who *did* want to go out with *me,* because I was a lucky bastard and Lily was a bit of a rebel, at least when it mattered.

When Mackenzie finally got to his feet, I did as well. Other people were starting to glance at me (and Fat Guy was practically trembling with the urge to confront me) and with my antennae being so hypersensitive at the moment, I knew I didn't want to sit there after my mate had gone. I couldn't do it. Mackenzie was like an unwitting bodyguard. My protector, my shield, my veil of impunity—and anyway, I was going to leave before I started having doubts about my sexuality.

"So I'll see you later," he said.

"Yeah, grand," I said. And I don't know why it happened, but I suddenly needed to suck in a big lungful of air, like I'd been thumped in the chest. And having breathed in, I blurted it out on the exhale: "I'm sorry."

"What?"

"That thing, that joke. I'm sorry I did it, like. Stupid. Sorry."

"Oh, that. Right. Yeah." He shifted uncomfortably, then grinned at me. "See you later then."

"Uh-huh."

I'd said it, I'd said it. I hadn't said it to Joanna Ricks, but that was impossible. I hadn't said it to her family, but that was only theoretically possible in one of those parallel universes. I hadn't said it to Aoife Connor, First Accuser and Screenshotter, but that was *never* going to happen.

But I said it. I felt better. Kind of better. I felt lighter.

There was a card in the window and I could read it backwards: something about Hiring Now: Vacancies Available. I turned impulsively to the barista behind the counter and said. "You're hiring?"

She gave me a very straight look, and her mouth twisted just a little at the edges.

"No," she said.

Gillian Philip

9

Like a dog unto its vomit, isn't that what they say? That's what it was like, the way I kept going back to Twitter. I stayed off Facebook, but I didn't delete my account. I hadn't looked at my Friends list for days, and I wanted to put off the moment as long as possible, and besides, the contempt of international strangers was more palatable than what my ex-friends would be saying about me.

They were pretty international by now, the strangers. What was it Sid had said about a slow news day? It was clearly a slow news day in Taiwan, where an enterprising young animator had made a cute little 90-second film based on a coyote (I think it was a coyote) getting thrown off a train by a couple of Scottish lions. I mean, why on earth did he care? He'd dubbed the iPhone footage into Taiwanese, or whatever. I found myself strangely detached from that one; so much so that I could quite admire the artistry. The coyote was pretty cute, though I didn't think much of the castrated-chihuahua voice work.

Less cute was the photoshopped gif I found on Twitter, headed I FIXED YOUR JOKE FOR YOU. It wasn't funny. It wasn't funny because that was a picture off my own Facebook page. I was grinning and it wasn't a very good picture because one of my eyes was half shut, and I vividly remembered untagging myself from it. Also, I'd swiftly fixed my privacy settings after the whole mess had started, so how had they got hold of it?

It also wasn't funny because a barrel of chemicals (helpfully labelled CHEMICALS) whooshed out of left-screen and took my head clean off, with a dramatic splatter of paintbox-blood.

Everybody else thought it was funny. Everybody else thought it was twenty-six-crying-with-laughter-emojis funny. Bar a couple of disapproving tuts from middle-aged people who had no business being on social media, it was all LOLS and ROFLs and PMSLs. And when it wasn't those, it was the guy who said IF I EVER FIND THIS FUCKER I WILL RIP HIS HEAD OFF AND I WONT NEED A BARRLE.

I set my phone down gently on the table and took a moment to get my breath. Look, I *know* it was Twitter and I *know* it wasn't real life, but you try keeping your stomach from turning sideways when somebody promises to behead you, and without the help of a flying barrle (I mean *barrel*). There were journalists and politicians who were probably so used to it that they didn't even notice it any more—and there was probably quite a bit of evidence of that on the laptop now in police custody, I'm embarrassed to say—but it was my first time. I was a

Twitter Abuse Virgin and my skin wasn't all that thick.

I thought: *Oh God Lily's seeing all this.* I didn't for a minute imagine that she wouldn't be looking. I could no longer imagine a world where people I knew *and most especially Lily* were not slavishly following every word written to, for and about me. I wondered what she'd be thinking. I wondered how she felt about it. It was an extremely brief thought process between wondering, and deciding I had to find out.

Nothing else was important. Why hadn't this struck me before? She was only not-messaging me because she didn't know how I'd react, she was worried about me, she was sensitive about what had happened, and what it meant for me. Everything else—the police investigation, the continued pestering from Jack Michie and sundry less obsessed hacks, and my fairly urgent need to find a job— faded like the blurred background on a moving selfie. Everything would be a whole lot better if I could just see Lily.

I couldn't drive, not in the Painted Vauxhall, so I walked. The Cumnocks didn't live too far out of town. Brodie had built himself a beautiful, shining, sprawling house just two miles beyond the outskirts of Langburn, and he'd bought enough of the surrounding land to make sure nobody else did the same. There were paddocks on two sides, a cluster of outbuildings and a long, long garden that stretched as far as the burn on the edge of the woods. You never saw Brodie sweating over a lawnmower, but the grass was green and stripy and edged with elegantly curving borders full of the sort of plants they put around showhomes to save maintenance and mess. Closer to the house were neat herbaceous borders edged with rabbit wire. Picture-fecking-perfect.

There was no sign of a human being as I slouched towards the drive, and I didn't know whether to be glad or sorry. I wanted to see Lily—God, did I want to see Lily—but if there was any sign of Brodie's car approaching, I'd have to dive behind a tree. And the trees were all neatly-staked saplings.

I was starting to sweat, and my hands prickled. The everybody-is-staring-at-me thing apparently still operated when there was no-one around to stare. I picked up my pace till I'd reached the back of the house (as shiny as the front) and I ducked behind one of the garages. Then I stood with my back against it, palms hard against the pristine bricks, till my heart had settled down a bit.

If I looked to the left I could see a sliver of paddock beyond a white ranch fence. I could see a slice of Pontchartrain, too, noble head cropping the grass. The big brute flicked an ear back, raised his head (still chewing), and turned. My breath stopped, and Lily walked into frame.

I'd started jogging towards her before I could think better of it. I was jogging on tiptoe, and on shaking legs, but I still almost ran right into view. I stopped in the nick of time when I saw who was in the adjacent yard.

Brodie's back was turned to me because he was polishing his blue Mercedes, but I skidded to a halt and stumbled into the shadow of a gigantic tree that must have predated the house by a century or two. Lily started at the movement and straightened, peering against the sun's glare.

I didn't show myself straight away. Her brown hair was haloed in a glow of golden sun, and warm fuzzy shadows fell on her cheekbones. I heaved an involuntary breath at her sheer beauty. She glanced furtively back at her father, then, more anxiously, at me. She bit her bottom lip, adorably. Even in muddy jeans, she looked as glossy and expensive as Pontchartrain.

She said something to her father. He said something back, and she laughed. I couldn't hear what either of them said, but I already resented her for laughing at my tormentor's jokes. *Maybe he said something about me.* My heart squeezed.

We went through a lot to get where we are. Lily Lily Lily don't let me down. God, I should be writing songs for boybands.

"Bye," she called, and in my head she was saying it to me. So I was almost surprised when she marched across to the fence, hopped elegantly over it and hurried over to where I stood.

I wasn't too shocked to lurch towards her, licking my bottom lip before I could help myself. (Creepy or what?) She kind of flinched, but then she blinked and accepted a kiss. Because it was only acceptance, I backed away in a hurry.

"What are you *doing*?" she whispered, her eyes wide. She grabbed my arm. "My Dad'll kill you."

"I had to see you," I said, like I was taking dialogue from a soap.

"You have to get out of here."

"You haven't messaged me." Pathetic.

"I will, I will." She risked another look over her shoulder. "Please, Eddie, you'll get in trouble."

"I've got in trouble with him before," I whispered.

"But it's different now. It's worse."

"Everything's worse." Oh, *get a grip*.

"Yeah, and we'll have to sit it out. Wait a bit. Let it all calm down. You've got the police onto you, Eddie!"

"No *shit*. I didn't know that."

"Don't." Her eyes were all soft and pleading. "Don't get mad at me, *please*."

"Course not." Mad-at-Lily dissolved, leaving my insides humming for more contact. I clasped my hand over hers so that she couldn't take it away from my arm.

I had to clear my throat. "We're okay, right?"

"Yeah, course." She didn't meet my eyes. Oh God, this was bad.

"After everything. You know—"

"Yes, yes." She sounded almost impatient, but then she reached up and kissed me voluntarily. That was better. Wasn't it?

"I don't mean everything *now*, I mean everything—"

"*Yes Eddie*. You've got to go, you've got to go."

"Christ, really? Does he hate me that much?"

"He doesn't—" She licked her lips, and I wanted to intercept her tongue. "He's never actually *liked* you, Eddie. Is all. Like Flo…"

An invisible comment thread punched me in the gut. I wished she wouldn't mention Flo. I wished everybody would stop *mentioning Flo*.

But she had. "Like Flo didn't like you," I finished for her, "and we got past that, right?"

"Right." Lily nodded. She folded her arms. She tapped one booted foot. *Tapped her damn foot.*

Click Bait

"I love you, right," I told her.
She kissed me again, and actually smiled.
"I love you wrong."

Gillian Philip

10

What did that even *mean?* Was that the kind of clever-arsed retort they learned at Dunstane College? I absolutely hated Lily for the forty minutes it took me to slouch home, until I remembered how much I adored her, and how much effort it had taken to be allowed to do that. Once I remembered that, I had to do something to take my mind off the extreme physical urges that just made me want to lie in my room for hours. Getting a job would help with both that, and the need to retrieve my saved level in Lily's estimation. It had to be on her hard disk somewhere.

And Eddie, don't even THINK the word 'hard'.

Out of the sixteen inky bits of torn newsprint, I got myself three job interviews. I thought it was a result. Sometimes you don't get *any*.

It was a result till I showed up, anyway.

The two bars were a non-starter, in retrospect. I'm a good barman, but Brodie's a good actual man, and my reputation had travelled ahead of me. My hindsight was improving by the minute, and I realised fairly quickly that they'd given me the chance to show my face, either so that they could have a good look at it—then lock up their daughters—or for the sheer pleasure of telling me straight to it that I hadn't got the job.

The guy at the lumber yard was a little more sympathetic. Let's face it, I'm not just a willing worker, I *look* like one. I've got a certain amount of brawn and Lily says my forearms are particularly impressive. The guy knew I'd do a good job for him: I could tell by the reluctant expression on his face when he showed me the door. He was sorry he had to pass me up, that was obvious. But he was going to pass me up. I knew that before the shown-door closed on me. He must have seen the papers or the internet, some time between offering me the interview and seeing my nearly-broken nose in his office. Either that or he got The Call from the local business association chairman, and I'm sure I don't have to tell you *his* name.

But I didn't just trawl the small ads, oh no. They'd failed me—maybe the advertisers had had candidates in mind already; that did happen—and I'm all about taking the initiative, so I trudged round every pub in town. I checked out the bowling alley. I went into the council HQ and talked the blonde behind reception into giving me a list of vacancies. I wasn't quite dumb enough to apply for the caretaker vacancy at the local primary school, because I didn't think breaking the hearts of two primary-schoolers was going to look great on my CRB results, but I did submit myself for interrogation at the recycling centre.

Click Bait

It was the look of faint pity on the face of the supermarket manager that finally sent me home to reassess my strategy. Naturally, Sid was at the door when I arrived, and there was nothing faint about the pity on her face. She actually wrinkled her nose as she stepped back and let me turn the key.

And that was when I remembered Lily *flinching* when I'd leaned in to kiss her. My genitals shrivelled and blood hurtled to my face. *Oh. Jesus. Did I take a shower before I saw Lily?*

I actually couldn't recall. And given my current mood, I didn't much care. I was pretty sure I hadn't taken one in the three days since, which might have had something to do with my experience in the local job market. Surreptitiously I rubbed my tongue with my finger, and sniffed it. That was okay. I mean, I'm not a slob, I'd been brushing my teeth. There was only the faintest hint of Bacardi, and I kicked down the lid of the kitchen bin before Sid could possibly catch a glimpse of its contents.

She and I didn't exchange a word as I put on the kettle. Sid just leaned against the dresser (now why hadn't I taken that down to the recycling centre while I was going?) and played with Jesus Gerard Butler and his moveable arm while I searched fruitlessly for a packet of Bourbons. I had the horrible feeling she was psyching herself up to tell me something, and if Sid had to take a breath before opening her gob, it was never going to be what I wanted to hear.

"Have you got *any* food in this house?" she asked at last.

"There's definitely biscuits. I swear to God there's Bourbons here somewhere." I yanked open a drawer. It was the drawer with Blu-Tac, screwdrivers and lightbulbs, but I was getting desperate.

"I bet there's the other kind of bourbon," she said sniffily.

"What's that supposed to mean?"

She shrugged and picked at something caught in her braces. Half a badger, probably. "Eddie, can I make a suggestion?"

"Whatever."

"I mean, without you ripping my head off."

"Depends," I growled.

"Oh well, my head's never been that attractive anyway." She set Jesus Gerard Butler carefully back in his usual spot and folded her hands. "You're kinda letting yourself go, Eddie."

I slammed the drawer back into place. I straightened. I swore silently and took a deep breath, then gritted my teeth and turned to Sid. I said, "Fuck off."

"See, this is what I'm getting at. You used to swear with élan. You're not even trying any more." She scowled, which wasn't a good look on Sid. "Don't look at me like that. I'm trying to be positive."

"I haven't got any biscuits," I said, leaning back against the drawer and folding my arms.

"I don't want a sodding biscuit. I want you to fight back a bit. You smell like a hamburger."

She wanted to provoke me. I knew Sid well enough to know *that*. Trouble was, the only thing she was in danger of provoking was a crying jag.

"Don't you look like that. Don't you dare, Eddie. Don't you dare cry."

"Don't you dare think I might." I snatched up Jesus Gerard Butler, whose arm promptly fell off. "Oh, bloody hell." I tried to tear at my hair but it wasn't long enough. "Just drink your tea, Sid, for God's sake."

She went all demure, sitting down and picking out her teabag delicately with a spoon. In the silence I could hear the binbag window rattle in the breeze in the next room. This was as close as Sid and I had ever got to an awkward moment.

"What are the cops saying at the moment?" she asked, when I'd sat down opposite her and we'd had a suitable difficult silence.

"Uh." I couldn't help shivering. "Last I heard, they're going to charge me."

"For one joke?" Sid didn't look quite as disbelieving as I wanted her to.

"Well," I mumbled, "there was a bit more to it."

She stared at me.

"They found some comment threads on the laptop," I said, examining my knuckles. "Apparently they were kind of abusive. Bullying. Threatening, actually."

"Eddie? Eddie, that's not—that's not like you!"

I shrugged. "So that kind of exacerbates the whole thing, really. Means I've got form."

"I bet they don't really care about that. Not *really*."

"No, they're only annoyed cos I made a fantastically sick joke about somebody they loved. But every little helps, as they say at the Tesco that won't employ me."

Sid shoved back her chair and stood up. She licked her lips, then marched to the cupboard and pulled out that diminished roll of black plastic bags. How did she know where those were? I barely remembered myself. I was spending way too much time with Sidonie, and she was *way* too familiar with my house. Sadly, I didn't have the energy to tell her to go away.

She tore off a bag and started to fill it up from the pile of trash in the corner. I'd kind of forgotten the heap was there, but she was holding her breath as she stuffed cans and newspapers and sandwich wrappers into the black bag.

"I'm not kidding, Eddie. Get a grip. Nobody's going to employ you till you shave, for a start. And have a shower. Probably not in that order."

"You're really stroking my ego."

"I'm not trying to stroke your ego. Any minute now I'm going to slap you. Has that journalist been back?"

"Michie?" I sniffed. "Yeah. I'm not talking to him."

"You're not talking to anybody."

"He's still phoning the house. And he's not the only one." I picked a smidgin of Blu-Tac out of the packet, for something to do, rolled it into a ball and used it to re-attach Jesus Gerard Butler's arm. "I wish it would die down a bit."

"Slow news month. I warned you. Summer, Eddie. *Everybody* knows that."

We shared the kitchen for a moment in a silence that was slightly more comfortable. It was only broken when Jesus Gerard's arm fell off again with a muted click.

"Eddie, I want you to come out with me." Before I could even make my customary joke-objection, Sid had rolled her eyes. "And you know what I mean. You can't sit in here all day. You actually smell worse than the house."

Click Bait

Her cleaning-and-tidying route was taking her towards the pedal bin, so I quickly said, "Leave that, I'll get it."

She slanted her eyes suspiciously at the bin, which still wasn't properly closed, then shrugged. "You've got to face the world."

"I don't see why. I think I'll just wait for the court appearance and the jail sentence."

"You know nothing. If you go to court it'll just be a preliminary. You won't be going to jail for weeks. Months maybe. The sheriff's probably in Bali for the summer."

I glowered at her, silent and resentful. She sighed.

"I'm just spelling out the *possibilities*. I don't think you're going to jail at all."

"That's not what Officer Dibble told me."

"Officer Dibble was trying to wind you up, obviously. And what in God's name channel are you reduced to if you can find *Boss Cat*?"

I chewed the inside of my lip till it swelled. The truth was, I'd already been reduced to the QVC Shopping Channel; and the other truth was, I was sick of the sight of the wallpaper, never mind the TV. I glowered at Sid, hating her. "I'm not going anywhere with people in it."

"The whole point is to go somewhere with people."

"Well, I'm *not*."

"Baby steps, Eddie. Baby steps." Sid knotted the last black bag, slung it into the hallway, and tilted her head. "All right. We'll take the bus to Breakness and have a walk on the beach. Wouldn't you like that? Eh?"

I felt like her pet dog, the way she talked.

But I nodded.

11

I put on the baseball cap again and pulled it right down over my eyes before I was willing to be dragged to the bus stop. I thought about leaving my phone at home. I even tried to leave it; I really did. But my fingers trembled and twitched without it, and just as the front door was closing on us, I darted back inside and grabbed it off the dresser.

Armless Jesus Gerard gazed at me in disappointment. I ignored him.

Sid scowled, but she followed it up with a beatific smile. "The bus just went up the road," she told me, jerking a thumb. "It'll be at the terminus and back in three minutes."

"Great," I mumbled. And I kind of meant it, because the bus stop was right opposite Number 44, and the curtains were already twitching. I didn't know how long I could make myself stand there without grabbing a brick and pitching it at Number 44's ornamental birdbath.

"Nobody's looking, Eddie."

I realised Sid was watching me with an expression of real concern. "I know that."

"They're really not. They're all watching the footie on the TV, Eddie."

"Right," I said, unconvinced.

"I'm not kidding. They care about the match a lot more, Eddie. They've got short attention spans, you know."

I nodded. "Whatever."

She sighed, and stuck out a hand for the returning bus. You didn't have to stick out your hand—if they saw you, they stopped—so the gesture gave the lie to all her reassurances. She didn't think the driver would stop for me. She thought he'd drive on. He *would* have driven on. I grabbed the handrail and hung on as if I could hold the bus back.

As we climbed in, Sid twisted her head and gave me a stare that went right through me. Her comment wasn't so understanding. "Jesus, Eddie!"

I hated how Sid was psychic and everything. I pulled the peak of my hat even further down my face, and grunted and flashed my card, and the driver pretended not to look at me. Well, he didn't look at me, but I *knew* that was only when I was watching him.

Halfway down the bus, I swung into a vacant aisle seat (they were all vacant, thank God), to make sure Sid couldn't sit beside me. Sid plonked herself down in the seat across the aisle.

"Nobody *cares*," she hissed as the bus pulled away.

I stared out of the window. I wondered if she was right. I doubted she was right. I wasn't sure I wanted her to be right. If my life was in shreds, there had to be a bloody good reason for it and I didn't see why I should suffer alone.

The closer we got to Breakness, the worse I felt. Nobody was getting off the bus, but at every stop there were two or three getting on. Most of them didn't spare me a glance, but an old guy, his missus, and one pregnant woman glared right at me. I only realised she might have an ulterior motive for glaring when the old guy got stiffly to his feet and offered her his seat in a notably loud voice.

Oh well. By that time I was sunk so far down into the scratchy purple fabric, I doubt I could have got up anyway.

I got up fast enough when the bus rocked to a halt, shooting to the front and jumping down the steps. Sid wasn't right behind me, because she was more polite, but she caught up soon enough by dodging pushchairs and walking sticks and a huge beach ball carried by a five-year-old. And the five-year-old. When she fell into step at my side she was panting a little.

"Tourism's picking right up," she offered by way of a conversation starter. "No wonder. Kinda hot. Take your jacket off."

I turned up its collar. "No."

"You're off your head," she said. "I'll buy you an ice cream then."

"I'm not going in the shop," I told her with a magnificent lack of grace.

"Fine," she snapped.

Maybe Sid was getting sick of me too; I was certainly giving her cause. I wasn't entirely unhappy with that. If I pissed her off enough, she might stop nagging me to rejoin the world of the living, and besides, I wasn't sure any more how to deal with blatant niceness.

I slouched across the road to the Dot Cumming Memorial Park, the one that overlooked the dirty estuary, and sat on a bench till I saw Sid from the corner of my eye, walking out of the Mermaid Cafe with a couple of cones. She stopped and looked around, and I flicked the peak of my cap up slightly, crooking a surreptitious finger. I distinctly saw her roll her eyes as she caught sight of me.

She sat down just a little too close, and passed me a cone.

"The red tulips are late to bloom on the banks of the Volga," she said.

"Ah shut up."

"Well, honestly. You're not in a bleedin' spy novel. Take your jacket off. You're more conspicuous with it on. People are staring."

I thought about it. I peered to left and right. There was a sweaty woman in a flowery dress on the next bench along; her own cone had paused halfway to her pink lips as she gaped at me.

"Fair enough." I handed Sid the cone, shrugged off my jacket, and took it back. I realised I was kind of sweaty myself. "You didn't get me a flake."

"You are a flake," said Sid, childishly.

The dirty estuary was looking its best, I had to admit, with sun shards glittering on the water and the upstream river as blue as the sea and the sky. It wasn't actually dirty; it just looked that way most days, what with the cast-up seaweed and the little fringes of stiff yellow scum. A kid with a shrimp net was screaming its purple face off as its father tried to coax it past the weed and the scum into the water.

"Go round to the actual beach," I grunted under my breath, "and don't be so bloody lazy."

The beach and the dunes, though, could only be reached across a rickety wooden bridge, and you had to make a bit of an effort. I wouldn't have done it myself.

"Will we go over to the beach?" asked Sid the mind-reader.

I shook my head, and she shrugged. We chewed on soggy bits of cone, and I watched the bridge. A family was struggling across it with a coolbox and a windbreak and lumpy plastic bags full of toys, and they were about to meet a bunch of lads right in the middle of the bridge. The lads were typically boisterous, shoving each other as they approached the family, but within a couple of metres of them, their six-foot-three leader lifted an arm and made them all press back to let the human camels pass.

I knew exactly how tall he was. It wasn't a guess. Only Drew Hunter was that ostentatiously polite, anyway. I tried to shrink tighter against the bench, but I couldn't take my eyes off the group as it made its way across the estuary and down the path towards the park. I felt Sid grab my hand, and I shook her off furiously.

"Hiya, Sid." Drew Hunter did *everything* ostentatiously, including pretending-I-didn't-exist.

Sid nodded, watching him over her cone with narrowed eyes.

I wasn't looking at Drew any more. I was looking at Mackenzie, and I had a horrible feeling my gaze was a beseeching one. Mackenzie himself was kind of avoiding my eyes. He stuck his hands in his pockets and laughed at something nobody had even said. Drew had turned away from Sid and was focused on me now, but it was my turn to pretend *he* wasn't there.

They were in a sort of semicircle in front of us now, just rocking back and forward on their heels, grinning at each other, grinning at Sid, not-grinning at me.

"Nice day," said Drew to Sid. "Bad luck about the company."

"Piss off, Drew," said Sid, giving him a Look.

He didn't even flinch. "I was going to pretend there was a really bad smell around, but I don't even have to pretend. Fwaugh!"

"How do you spell that?" asked Sid, flashing him a metal smile.

"D-O-O-L—"

"Oh, give it a rest, Drew," sighed Sid, slumping back against the bench.

"Does he not talk?" asked Owen Gregor, getting his guts together all of a sudden.

I wanted to kill him. I wanted to kill them all. A tight spasm of rage went through my chest and I blurted, "Said I was sorry."

There was a pained silence. Everybody stared at me. Including the melting fat woman in the flowery dress on the next bench. Well, that came out louder than I meant it to.

"Oh aye?" purred Drew. "When?"

I nodded savagely at Mackenzie. "Him," I said, "I said it to him."

Mackenzie looked at an azalea.

"Oh right, then, not to Jo." Drew's mouth tugged up at the corner. "Not to Jo's kids, like."

I stood up before I could stop myself. "I'm hoping Jo's kids haven't seen it, if you haven't feckin' *shown it to them.*"

"Aye, I wouldn't show that to innocent kids." Red spots appeared on Drew's cheekbones. "And she's not *Jo* to you, she's *PC Ricks*. It's like I said, you scum-sucker, you're needing to apologise to this whole town."

"What, Breakness?" God, Drew Hunter really brought out the arse in me. "Right, I'm sorry, right? Now fuck off."

Drew smirked, exchanging a glance with the increasingly-uncomfortable Mackenzie. "Mack told us you were sorry, actually. Aye, I bet you are. Sorry for yourself. Sorry you got found out. Sorry you've shown yourself up for a dirty arsewipe."

Owen cackled. Mackenzie was starting to smile. I dearly, dearly wanted to hit him. *You were my mate. Mine.*

You ran to your other mate and told on me, you shitstain. You told him. You told him I was sorry.

Which was fine, till I can imagine youse all laughing.

My nails were digging into my clenched palms and I was grinding my teeth hard enough to break them. I knew I couldn't stand this. I knew I had to do something. God, *anything*. So I actually opened my mouth to apologise again, and this time I'd grovel, I'd plead, I'd *make it stop*. Which was when it actually struck me.

They didn't want me to be sorry. I could apologise till my pride was in a filthy puddle on the tarmac and it wouldn't make a difference. They didn't want me sorry, they wanted me gone. They wanted me out of Langburn and Breakness and preferably Glassford as well. They wanted me to stop existing. They'd done their bit and they had probably had enough now, they were probably bored of the whole thing, but I was still here, and that wasn't a very satisfying outcome. It would be satisfying if I wasn't around any more. It was a good story for them to tell, over and over and online and every Friday night, but the ending didn't wrap things up and one of the characters was not supposed to be around at the final credits. I was an embarrassing awkwardness. Langburn-and-district was way too small a place to accommodate the dregs and the leftovers and they wanted me not to be there any more. They didn't want to make it stop. They wanted to make *me* stop.

"Fuck off," I said out loud. "I'm not gonnae stop."

Marvellous. Bloody marvellous. That came out well.

12

I walked with Sid along the top of the harbour wall. On one side of me, three feet down and not far enough, was pitted tarmac, splashed with broken patches where Victorian cobbles showed through. On the other side was sloshing, sucking water that wasn't deep enough. I did stop and I did shuffle my toes out over the browny-green water and narrow my eyes and imagine plunging in there—*Get In The Sea*, as they say on Twitter—but it would be a pretty unconvincing way to drown myself, and really undignified to have Sid drag me out by the ankles.

Besides, I didn't want to drown myself. It wasn't that bad. Yet.

"You could have put that a *lot* better," said Sid, leaning out and stretching her arms back like Kate Winslet on the Titanic. "What did you mean, *I'm not going to stop*?"

"Not what they think I meant," I growled.

She looked precarious, which I think was intentional. Grabbing an arm would knock her off balance, so I clenched and unclenched my fists, gritted my teeth, and yanked her back by the waist. She smirked a little, and I let her go.

"Well," she stated-the-bleeding-obvious, "whatever you meant, it didn't sound good."

"Oh, no shit. What it sounded like was: I'm going to continue to post tasteless and borderline illegal jokes about tragically brave victims with happy marriages and small children, and there's nothing you can do to stop me."

Sid folded her arms and nodded. "That's a very articulate summary, Eddie. Which makes me wonder why you can't be a little more articulate around your mates."

"Shut up."

"See what I mean?"

"And they're not my mates." In a mutter I added, "Not any more."

"Uh-huh. I must say, Mackenzie Clark is a prize shit."

"Thank you." I felt slightly better. I sat down on the wall. The stone was cold despite the heat of the day, and its greenish film was a permanent dampness that started soaking into my jeans right away. "What am I supposed to do, Sid?"

She didn't reply. When Sid doesn't answer, there isn't an answer.

I yanked my phone out of my pocket, and prodded at the screen.

"Don't do that, Eddie," she blurted.

I gave Sid a sideways glare. She looked away, embarrassed.

"I see," I said.

Mackenzie was off my Friends list. Well, there was a surprise. Even as I thought it, I knew it *would* have been a surprise, if I'd checked it forty minutes ago. But Mackenzie was either not bright enough to make his page private, or he wanted me to see it. And it was his usual endearing mix of emojis, bad spelling and football till I checked the photos.

I recognised most of the shots, because I used to be in them. It was fine, though. It wasn't physically possible to feel any sicker, so I was quite numb as I went through his albums. *T in the Park Festival! Glassford Senior Schools League Winnerzzzzzz! OWENS 18th YA BAMS! Fuengirola 2015!*

He'd cropped me out of every one. You could occasionally see an arm, or the edge of my jaw, but I swear to God, there wasn't enough of me to tag any more. The only shot of me that had survived the massacre was a blurred and tiny face at the back of the Glassford Academy 2nd XI official team photo.

I clicked back to the Fuengirola album. It had been hard work cropping me out of those, because we were usually in a tight (manly) hug or he was flopped across my legs in a pile in the sand, or I'd been sagging against him with a beer in my hand. I didn't feel any sicker, sure, but I got an abrupt lance of sheer hurt right through my ribcage.

I hated Mackenzie Clark right then. You know what I wanted? I wanted him to stop.

*

Fuengirola.

We'd got dirt-cheap last minute flights on Easyjet to Malaga and we decided to go on the spur of the moment, because school was only just out forever, and you've got to enjoy life before you settle down into that nice secure job that's waiting for you. I barely had time to tell Flo where I was going. I checked my passport was up to date, I packed, I bought a new pair of sunglasses. The lads arrived in a horn-hooting taxi at four-thirty in the morning, waving blearily, yelling at me to hurry up, ignoring the twitching curtains at number 44. I kissed Flo goodbye—her still half-asleep with last night's mascara smudged on her eyelids—and we caught the plane by the skin of our teeth.

I had a good time on that holiday. I was only on it for a day and a half, but what there was of it was just about the most fun I'd ever had. There were (or there used to be) pictures of me and Mackenzie by the hotel pool, and a photo of me throwing him into it. There was a photo of the four of us in bad sun hats, drinking bad cocktails in a bad bar. (That's me, Mackenzie, Owen and his brother Marty. Even then I wasn't friends with Drew Hunter.) Every single picture, we were grinning our heads off. We couldn't believe the heat. We couldn't believe the cheap alcohol. We couldn't believe the freedom.

If Flo hadn't had the heart attack, I'd have been there for a week, but what the hell. Even thirty-six hours was better than a slap in the face with exam revision.

See, it wasn't like I could leave Flo to die alone and scared. My God, was she scared. She sounded terrible on the phone, and terrified. She needed me, she was desperate for me. There wasn't anything I could do but call the airline, get my flight changed (at more cost than the original ticket) and fly home to be with her.

Not that Flo actually died, not that time. Luckily it was a false alarm. And even for a false alarm, I'd never have been able to live with myself if I'd stayed in Fuengirola for a week, drinking cocktails and turning my initial lurid sunburn into a decent tan.

At least Flo didn't die alone.

Not that time.

Its a crying shame that anybody dies alone, Eddie. Nobody deserve's that.

Give it a rest, Flo.

Gillian Philip

13

The Procurator Fiscal was not in a forgiving mood, apparently. He charged me by recorded delivery mail, and not just for the Facebook joke but for several other incidents of malicious communication, as revealed by that laptop and its infuriatingly intact hard disk.

There was a helpful template letter in the envelope, so I could plead guilty by return post. Snarling defiance to no-one in particular, I pleaded not-guilty and shoved it in the nearest postbox.

I'd never imagined being a hardened criminal could be so dull. I felt like all I'd done was sign up for a crash course in legal terminology. The Intermediate Diet date was a little closer than I liked; it seemed I was on a fast track to hell (never mind the boy bands; I could be writing for a thrash metal combo) so I found the bookmark for the Legal Aid page, filled in the online boxes and only just stopped myself claiming Crow as a dependant. The first two firms on the list were too busy—and me a celebrity!—but number three took me on.

Martin Innes of Cockburn & Imrie was under-impressed by my not-guilty plea.

"Eddie," he said. He pushed his glasses up his nose and peered at the charge sheet and sighed a lot. "I don't see much in the way of extenuating circumstances, to be honest. I'd recommend you plead guilty at the Intermediate Diet. That'll be your last chance to, um. To suck up to the court, basically."

"I might think of something," I said, and dug my heels in. "Can I plead guilty at the last trial if it goes that far?"

He pushed his glasses again; they kept slipping down. "It won't make any difference by the Trial Diet."

'Yeah but anyway."

See? I was a dab hand at the legal bit now. *Yeah but anyway.*

The next time I saw him, I had regrets about being so bolshie. Strutting his stuff in the Sheriff Court, he looked a good bit more intimidating than he had over his desk. I had to kick my brain and remind myself he was *on my side*.

It was a cloudless, brilliant Friday morning and the smokers were out on the courthouse steps, basking in Vitamin D before they had to go and sew mailbags or whatever. There were tab ends squashed into every crack in the concrete. I didn't pause for a last smoke myself because Jack Michie's constantly-silent photographer was there, giving me a friendly smile and a thumbs-up as he lowered his camera. *God.* He might have asked me to smile, or pull my stomach in or something. I was pretty sure those shots were not going to be very flattering.

Jack Michie himself was inside the building, looking smirky and faintly desperate. "All right, Eddie! Any chance of a comment yet?"

I grunted, and turned desperately on my heel in search of a distraction. And on cue there was Martin Innes behind a big glass door, shoving coins into an uncooperative coffee machine and swearing under his breath: I could read his lips. He glanced up and smiled and nodded, and as soon as the machine grudgingly came up with a brown paper cup, he swept through the glass door towards me.

He really did sweep. He was wearing a black gown that made him look like Professor Snape with a crewcut.

"Hello, Eddie. That's your door." He jerked a thumb. "You can just sit in the public seating till your case comes up. Listen out for your name and number. You're 35. I'll be down the front." He gave me a quick recap of the instructions he'd given me in the office, glanced at his watch, downed the coffee in one and vanished through a different door.

I pushed open the public door, which creaked horribly, but nobody turned to look at me. God, the courtroom looked formal, and God, I felt queasy. There was wood panelling and an elaborate coat of arms above the sheriff's long bench. There were high arched windows, uncurtained. There was a hatless police officer sitting on a chair to the side, looking bored. There were a *lot* of men in black robes. There was an ornate plaster ceiling painted blue-and-white, and the public benches behind the dock were like ancient church pews. On the bright side, the waiting defendants of decades had amused themselves carving graffiti into the back of the benches in front of them. *Spud. Marty xxx. ALLY + DECLAN. Nathan B*

4 Evah. I swear there were names I recognised, and some wag had carved a crude cock-and-balls that was too recent to have been obliterated. It kind of cheered me up.

It cheered me up until a red-headed woman marched in and barked, "Court rise," and everybody had to stand up *like this was actually serious*, and the sheriff breezed in in black robes and white tie and an actual *wig*.

Oh, God oh God oh God. I'd fallen into an episode of Judge John Deed, and I wasn't the good guy.

I'd picked the bench furthest from the dock and I sat there for three-quarters of an hour, feeling less special by the minute. A 90-year-old who didn't want to stop driving, my lord, despite that incident with the pram, and his GP was fine with it. A straggle-haired biker type who hadn't paid his fine (I couldn't hear what for; they murmured a lot). A guy in a blue hoodie, brought from the cells handcuffed to a hot G4S security woman (I shouldn't be noticing the hotness of the guards). A woman in a pink hoodie who was in the habit of helping herself to nail polish; and she was very keen, my lord, to be given another opportunity to prove herself (the sheriff wore Unconvinced Face, which was pretty terrifying in this context). There were long silences while the sheriff read submissions, or the solicitors whispered to their clients. Martin Innes represented four other people while I watched. The sun was glaring through the uncurtained windows straight into my eyes.

I blinked hard and glanced at the clock on the wall. Nobody said I had to sit through everybody else's crimes and misdemeanours. I edged out of the seat, creaked open the door and went outside for a fag.

My timing sucked. I wasn't halfway through my cigarette when I heard the booming voice.

"Edmund Doolan. EDMUND DOOLAN."

I dropped the half-fag as if I'd burned my fingers, and raced back inside. The Bored Hatless Policeman was just vanishing back into the court, announcing "No appearance, my lor—"

I bolted in at his heels, blurting "Sorry! Sorry."

Martin Innes shot me a glance that held all the long-suffering in the world, and turned to his papers. "Edmund Doolan. Number 35."

The sheriff nodded to me with a faint exasperated smile. "Mr Doolan. Have a seat please."

I shot into the dock. I felt dizzy enough to throw up, but I didn't think that would go down too well. Martin Innes was talking already, but I swear I heard nothing but a kind of underwater echo.

"Mr Doolan, you wish to plead Not Guilty, is that right?" The sheriff was looking at me very formally, playing with his pen.

I nodded, muttered something in the affirmative. I could hardly breathe and I was sweating from my panicked run. The sheriff talked. Martin Innes talked again. He flicked his black robe back, adjusted it on his shoulders. He picked up another paper. He was talking. The sheriff was talking.

"Mr Doolan. *Mr Doolan?* Will you stand up, please?"

I wasn't sure I could, but I tried anyway and found I could get myself upright. They were all being so *polite.* The sheriff had a friendly sort of face. *It couldn't be that bad.*

And before I could even tune in to listen properly, Martin Innes was smiling fixedly at me and shoo-ing me with one hand.

I stumbled out of the dock and marched back past the public benches. I yanked open that ridiculously creaky door and scurried into the lobby, fumbling for my cigarettes. Martin Innes strode through a gaggle of men in black robes, already rooting beneath his own robe for more change for the coffee machine.

"All right, Eddie, you get that? Trial Diet on the 23rd of this month." He pushed his glasses up his nose and counted his bits of change. "Put it in your diary! *The 23rd.* Behave yourself, laddie. And don't forget the trial or you're toast."

I nodded as he gave me a cheerful wave and turned towards the coffee machine. I turned, shoved through the entrance doors and gasped in a lungful of free air. The free air didn't quite hit the spot, so I lit another cigarette with trembling fingers.

I'd had vague visions of being escorted to a cell by men with plumed hats, britches and pikes, so it all felt like a bit of an anticlimax. Well, until Jack Michie came bounding down the courtroom steps, photographer at his heels.

I half-turned to tell him to go away; and he walked straight past me.

I could only stare after him, loose-jawed, as he climbed into his Skoda, scribbling on a pad. The photographer got into the passenger seat, and Michie pulled away.

What the actual? Was he bored with me? Nobody ever got bored enough with me. I found myself surprisingly offended. I might have been enduring Most Hated status, but at least it was a status. It was the only one I had going for me lately.

Click Bait

I stuck my hands in my pockets and glanced around the street. No howling mobs. No cameras. I got a few looks as pedestrians walked past the court, but I couldn't make out more than casual distaste.

That was good. Phew. What a relief.

Something a bit like resentment smouldered under my ribcage. I felt for a moment the way I'd felt on the bus to Breakness a few days ago. I still didn't know if I'd rather be villain or nobody, but I needed more time to decide. There'd been a moment when I'd thought I wanted to be nobody, but I wasn't ready to stop being, not yet. I didn't want to Stop.

I started walking down the High Street, as conscious of every bone and muscle and nerve in my body as everybody else was oblivious. It felt weird, like being in another dimension, but with a one-way mirror on the dimension wall.

So there were advantages to a small town. People might vandalise your car while you were out and tell tales behind your back to the papers, they might call you the Devil Incarnate on Facebook and corral you in the No-Job Zone, but they didn't follow you through town waving banners, they didn't organise flashmobs to the tune of *Shame On You*. It was fine. I was going to make it home without tar or feathers. I might even chance my arm and go for a Starbucks.

The downbeat optimism lasted till I was on the steps of Starbucks and the door opened. Megan the Dozy Barmaid was walking out, her and her gold-shellacked nails and her wage packet and her job security, and Fran Mitchell. Fran was the accountant at the Whistling Frog and I liked her. She liked me, because I was punctual and responsible and diligent and all the other things accountants tend to like. We used to have a laugh, me and Fran.

She didn't like me now. Her face froze. It should have stayed frozen. Instead her lips twisted down and her nostrils contracted and the flesh of her cheeks puckered. I couldn't see her backside but I'm sure it clenched.

"Are you not in jail yet?" she said, very loudly.

Megan puffed out a snort of amused disdain. Then they both swept past me like Tube train muggers, and marched off, ostentatiously not-looking-back.

People in Starbucks were staring. A few of them were whispering, and one or two laughed deliberately loudly. Distantly from my parallel dimension I heard the words *Jo* and *little boys* and *disgusting* and *filthy little abuser*. Strangely, it was *little* that stung the worst. Both times.

All right, I wanted to stop now.

I turned round and trotted as blithely as I could down the steps and headed home.

14

I was so not in the mood for Crow. I could see his scrawny distorted shape through the frosted side windows of the porch and I considered pretending I wasn't in. Instead I unhooked the door chain and opened the door a crack. No reporters in sight. Just Crow, Haribo-less. I opened the door wider and yanked him in.

"Bacon roll?" I said, walking through to the kitchen. "Or would you understand that better if I just said, 'Bacon roll'."

He didn't give me any sullen or insolent retort, which wasn't like him. My hackles instantly went up and I turned to look at him as he sloped into the kitchen after me. His hands were in his pockets and he was glowering at the lino.

"Sit down," I said, pulling out a chair and practically shoving him into it. He was still staring at the floor as if he could laser a hole in it, and his whole face was set in a tight scowl.

"Right," I sighed.

I let him sit there burning that hole in the lino while I fried yet more bacon and tore open slightly stale rolls with my fingers. I didn't have any butter, but that didn't seem to bother Crow. When I stuck two bacon rolls on a plate and put them in front of him, he just picked one up and sank his jaws into it.

"How long you need to stay?" I asked him.

He tilted his head to the side and shut one eye, calculating. At last he mumbled, "Hour maybe."

So, four hours minimum. His dad must be home. "Game of Thrones?" I suggested.

He made a face, his cheeks still stuffed with bacon.

"Walking Dead?"

Crow nodded eagerly, grabbing up his plate with the remains of the rolls and following me through to the lounge. I rooted out the DVD box set, picked a disc with some really gruesome episodes and slotted it into the player. For a while we sat on the sofa in concentrated silence. Marv padded into the room, gave the screen a dimwitted look of incomprehension, then jumped up onto the cushions between us, curled up against Crow's thigh and launched into a resounding purr. Crow managed to stop hugging himself so tightly, so that he could rub Marv's tummy.

The dull ache in my gut subsided and my brain shifted into numb-but-focused mode. Once or twice I actually winced and said "*Yuck,*" and pretended to cover Crow's eyes till he slapped me away and giggled. I knew there was a reason I put up with him.

Crow perked up a little as the hours and the episodes went by, to the point where his exclamations of disgust or fright became almost cheerfully obscene. So when he grew silent again, and I prised myself out of the sofa cushions and took the Coke can out of his limp hands, he only made a muted sound of protest.

"Shut up," I told him. I lifted Marv and plonked his limp body onto Crow's lap. The boy's arms instantly went round the cat, and he lay down on his side, dirty boots on the sofa, head on its arm. His eyes closed altogether and his mouth fell open. Marv was now stretched the length of Crow's concave torso, beside the boy rather than on him. The upholstery would be harder to wash than Crow's jeans, but I couldn't be bothered moving either him or the cat. Marv watched me through slitted eyes, daring me.

"Don't *you* dare *pee*," I growled.

Marv smirked, then yawned and closed his eyes. Sometimes I reckoned that cat was smarter than he made out.

When my phone buzzed in my pocket, I jumped. It had been so long, I swear I'd forgotten what it meant. Sid. Fumbling for it, I pulled it out and looked at the caller display.

Bloody hell, it was Lily.

I poked desperately at the not-very-sensitive screen, managing to answer just before it switched to voicemail. "Lily," I croaked. I cleared my throat. "Yeah, Lily?"

"Hey Eddie!" Her voice made my insides melt. I had to sit down on the edge of the sofa, next to Crow's feet. "Eddie, how are you? Are you okay?"

"Fine," I lied. "Fine."

Her voice turned soft. "I've missed you."

I coughed. "Missed you," I muttered.

"What's wrong? Why are you talking so quietly?"

"Got Crow," I said, glancing at him. "And Marv. Asleep. Crow is, I mean. Well, both of them."

"Oh, okay. Is he all right?"

"Crow or Marv?"

She giggled. "Crow."

"He's always all right."

"And Marv? Give him a kiss from me. Give him a tummy rub."

Yeah, but what about me, Lily? Where's my tummy rub? "Is your dad out. I mean, is your dad out?"

"I can tell you've been hanging out with Crow." Lily laughed again, which had always been the most beautiful sound in the world. "Yes, Dad's at some Rotary thing. God, Eddie, I've been following everything. It's been *awful.*"

Yes, Lily. Yes, it has. "It's okay now."

"Is it really? You had to go to court, right?"

"Yeah. Today. This morning." I hesitated, and the phone was horribly silent for long seconds. I couldn't hear her breathing or anything. "Are you there?"

"Yes, yes. Of course I am. Eddie, are you really all right?"

"*Yes.*" It came out with more irritation than I'd intended. "I'm okay, Lily." I paused. "Just kinda wish it was over. Y'know."

"It'll all calm down, Eddie. Honestly, it will."

"I need a job," I blurted.

"Oh God, I know, I know. I'm really sorry about that. Dad just—you know. He was really wound up about it for a few days. Thing is, he's pretty involved with the Glassford Police Welfare Fund. He was all—well, you can imagine."

Oh, I could imagine. *What did I tell you about that Doolan boy? A bloody thug, Lily. Waste of space. Not fit to lick your ninety-quid wellington boots.* Crow stirred a little, so I stood up and took the phone through to the kitchen. "Trouble is, Lily, I'm not getting a job in this town any time soon." One-handed I rummaged in the freezer for the vodka bottle and found myself a tumbler, and sat down at the kitchen table.

"Listen, Eddie, listen." She sounded breathless. "I haven't been forgetting you or anything. Honestly I haven't. I couldn't come and see you because—because he was mad at me and—well, I couldn't. But I'm working on him. All the time. I've been putting your case, Eddie. I think I might've talked him round. A bit, anyway."

I sloshed neat vodka into the tumbler and took a swallow. "How big a bit?"

She took an audible breath. "Do you think you could go see him? Maybe apologise?"

"Apologising hasn't got me very far lately."

"Oh. Oh. But—try him, will you?" I could imagine her pushing her fingers through her dark glossy hair, maybe nibbling on her nails in anxiety. It was killing me. "I think I've made a good case. Did you plead guilty?"

"No," I said.

"What?" There was another short silence. "Why?"

What could I say? I didn't actually know why. Panic? Resentment? A sliver of desperate hope that I could shirk all responsibility for the malicious communications? Possible onset of insanity? Martin Innes had looked at me as if he was coming down on the side of *crazy bastard*, but he'd just shrugged and taken my instruction. I couldn't say any of that to Lily, not on the phone, so I said nothing.

"Listen, Eddie. *Please.* Plead guilty, okay? They'll go easier, you never know. They might. And it'll all be over and—and you can talk to my dad."

"Talk. To your dad."

"*Yes.* I think he'll listen. I told him it was a spur of the moment thing, that I knew you were sorry, that you're a good guy. You *are* a good guy, Eddie." There were tears in her voice now, and it shook a little. "Eddie, I think he'd give you your job back."

That was almost enough to make me laugh. "You're sure. Huh."

"Pretty sure. Just talk to him, Eddie. He always liked you as—as an employee."

I gripped the tumbler hard and closed my eyes. *He always liked me. As an employee. As an employee.* "You're a—" I licked my lips. "You're optimistic."

"Try, Eddie. *Please.* Talk to him. I know we can sort this."

I said, "I'll think about it."

She sighed. I imagined her closing her eyes now. I pictured her tilting her head back a little, pursing her lips to blow out a silent breath: half frustrated but half relieved that she'd accomplished this much. "Thank you Eddie."

"He always liked me as an employee, eh?" I couldn't hold it back.

"You *know what I mean.* And it's not like your nan was mad about me. Come on."

"She always liked you," I began viciously, "as a—"

"As a what?"

I rubbed my forehead. "As a possibility," I muttered.

"A possibility, yes." Lily's voice took on an edge of frost. "Real-life me didn't work so well, but I guess she wouldn't like *any* real life girl who got her hands on you."

The thought of Lily's hands on me made me shudder—in a good way—but I managed to say, "That's not fair."

"Totally fair," she said crisply. "It's true and you know it."

I had another mouthful of vodka. I refilled the tumbler. God, I could not afford financially to drink this hard.

"Please," her voice said softly in my ear. "Don't let's fight. I'm sorry."

"Don't be sorry." The alcohol was giving me a sharp pain between my eyes. "You're right. Whatever."

"Flo was okay," said Lily, and I could imagine the effort it had taken her to say it. "You and I were fine in the end."

"I wouldn't go as far as *fine*," I said, and found myself laughing a little. With an edge of slight hysteria, sure, but it was a laugh. "We managed. We were okay."

"Better than okay." She was smiling again, I could hear it. Oh, thank God. "I did try to get on with Flo, Eddie. You know that, right?"

"Course."

"I've got to go," she said.

My stomach plummeted. "Okay."

"Talk to my dad, yeah?"

"Yeah," I lied. "Some time."

"Love you, Eddie."

And I just said, "Yeah."

*

Lily had done everything in her power to make Flo like her. Probably even more than I'd done to suck up to Brodie. I had to confess it was an achievement, a clear sign of Lily's determination.

I sat with my phone cradled in my hands, staring at its blank face and wondering why things didn't work the same way second time around. Lily and I fell in love against the wishes of our respective next-of-kin, we triumphed against the odds, we faced the whole Forbidden Love thing and we won. Now that things were *even worse,* you'd think we'd redouble our efforts and be twice as much in love as ever. Instead we were suddenly awkward and distant. I'd thought she was finished with me when she didn't contact me, but now that she had, I should be deliriously happy again. And I wasn't: I was anxious and edgy and I didn't know quite what to make of her breathless phone call.

It was a passing phase, was all. I didn't have a lot of spare space in my brain or my heart or my alternately numb and aching gut to focus on how much I loved Lily. And I *did.* How could I not?

Flo mistrusted her, because Flo loved me more than anything or anybody, but Lily tried never to let it get to her. Lily used to bring the old girl flowers and chocolates whenever she came round. She always remembered Flo hated carnations, so there were never carnations; there were roses and lilies and all the other things that made Tesco bouquets explode in price. She brought expensive chocolates, too, and Flo might have accepted them with a wide fixed smile, but that didn't stop her ravaging their ribboned boxes like an orc with a sweet tooth as soon as Lily left.

Lily sat in that lounge and asked Flo endless questions about her favourite daytime shows, and what it was like being an occupational therapist, and oh, where did she get her hair done, it was lovely. Lily had been amazingly good to her considering Flo hadn't actually had a *choice*. Flo *had* to accept Lily, and I'd told her so, loud and often. After all, it wasn't Lily's fault that Flo was bored. It wasn't Lily's fault that Flo retired too early, and didn't have a hobby beyond me, and couldn't get her hair done *every* day just for purposes of idle chat. Lily might not have helped the situation but it wasn't her fault that Flo was so unhappy.

It was me that should feel guilty about that, and I did. I was so much in love back then, I was blind to Flo's misery. I didn't notice the impending nervous breakdown, and I had Lily to think about (frequently, lustfully), and I had a job at one of her father's bars that took up a *lot* of time and, let's face it, a *lot* of emotional attention in the form of sucking-up to the boss.

So when, out of the blue, Flo mixed herself a gin-and-Xanax cocktail and lay down to die, I was as shocked as anyone else.

Luckily, the cocktail was ineffectual. I came home in time, and she hadn't known enough about quantities to do real damage (or much damage at all, despite the copious vomit), and they detoxified her at A&E (not having to resort to the stomach pump, thank God) and sent her home with a free pack of paracetamol and that was it. They seemed relatively relaxed about it and said it wasn't a serious attempt, and they'd contact her GP to recommend stronger anti-depressants. Coming so soon after the heart attack scare, I suppose Flo's death-wish had been blunted, and just as well.

But how could I be sure? The shock kept me at her side, watching her every move, for days. If Lily couldn't understand that, it was Lily's problem.

Because Lily and I had a major falling-out about it, owing to Lily's casual use of the words *attention-seeking*. We didn't speak for a week, and I thought we were finished; instead she apologised as only a Dunstane College girl can apologise. We were reconciled in a touching and desperately lustful scene down the alley beside the Whistling Frog after my Saturday evening shift.

And Flo, still teary and shocked and recovering, was fine about us getting back together. She cried and said she'd been a silly old woman, and she'd just been so unhappy that evening, and she'd been afraid she was losing *everybody*. But she understood how much I loved Lily and she really only wanted me to be happy and she was so glad.

Really she was.

15

Twitter, eh? In hindsight, #SickBastardsForEddie was an inevitability.

A few right-on journalists and commentators had my back now, and quite honestly they might as well have stuck a knife in it. Their campaign to have me forgiven and forgotten continued to be drowned out by the death threats and the DISGUST (routinely capitalised), but it also served as extra oxygen for the outrage. And Twitter did not appear to be subject to the same live-case rules as the press (yes, I'd finally found out why Jack Michie was ignoring me)—or if it was, it had decided to disregard the exasperated tweets of legal experts.

#SickBastardsForEddie is quite a lot of characters, especially when combined with #FreeSpeech, but it's amazing how concise a stomach-churning joke can be. Loads of tweeters were playing the game, and it was whipping the DISGUSTED people into a frenzy of frustrated hatred.

More than #SickBastards was winding them up. The internet being what it is, Marv was no longer the only cat in my life. There was a whole meme dedicated to #CatsReactToEddiesHead, and they had been helpfully collated (by a journalist with too much time on his hands) into a Buzzfeed article: 'Somebody Made A Sick Joke, And The Cats Of Twitter Turned It Into A Meme.'

I sat on the back doorstep, swiping my finger monotonously across my phone to refresh the page. Top to bottom, top to bottom. I showed Marv a few of the cat gifs and photos, but mostly he just purred resoundingly between my feet, giving a fly an occasional slap that always missed.

I sighed. It was nice of the Guardian's Ewan Madsen to disapprovingly retweet a threat (to stuff a chemical barrel down my throat and set light to it), but it still gave the tweet an extra outing, and as a respected national journalist, he had nearly 80,000 followers. Just as well Mr Madsen hadn't seen the note posted through my letterbox this morning; my death was going to be a lot slower than the chemical barrel one, if that particular moonbat had their way.

I did wonder why I was sitting on the back doorstep, exposed to the castration knife of a stalking lunatic, but all the loathing and all the death threats had formed a chaotic ball of howling voices in the back of my skull, and they'd stopped meaning very much. I reached down to tickle the back of Marvin's head.

"Should I tweet I'm sorry, Marv?"

He rolled his head back and gazed at me. Cats can look thick and contemptuous simultaneously.

"That's a No, then."

He stretched ecstatically, and started to purr again.

Marvin was right. If I tried to apologise it would only give the whole thing another kick forward. Nobody would accept I was sorry anyway, not going by Drew Hunter and Mackenzie Clark. Nobody wanted an apology, I reminded myself. They wanted me to *stop*.

I opened up the *Mail Online* again. The picture of me, outside the sheriff court before the hearing, was terrible. You could see Martin Innes's arm and his folder, but otherwise I filled the frame. My eyes glinted evilly from the shadow under the baseball cap, and my mouth was sulky. My hands were shoved in my pockets as I climbed the steps, and my shoulders were hunched. And I was slightly blurred, which always looks shifty. What a ned. What a thug.

"I'm going to have to do it, amn't I?" I asked Marv.

He twitched his ears and blinked at me resentfully.

"I haven't got any money left," I told him. "My overdraft is spectacular and I'm running out of cat food, apart from anything else. Lily's right. I'll have to throw myself on Brodie's mercy."

Marv purred out a squeaky sigh through his nostrils, and patted my foot with his paw.

Yes, Eddie. Yes, you are.

*

From the street, Brodie Cumnock's office was one of those huge houses from about a hundred years ago, with a garden that had been entirely turned over to a lock-block parking surface. Well, except for the shrubs at the edge, which were the same low-maintenance prickly things he had edging his lawn at home. The huge board at the front fence said CUMNOCK PROPERTIES GLASSFORD LTD. You really couldn't miss it. I was running out of time and excuses.

There was a bus stop right outside the entrance and I waited at it for a while, sweating cold blood, pretending I'd got there by accident. A bus stopped for me, and when I shook my head, the driver shook his head too, rolled his eyes, and pulled away. I really couldn't stand here forever.

When I finally got the courage to walk through the gateway and across the car park, I was shaking. The door was a massive wooden thing, and as it turned out, it wasn't the door. Only when I'd yanked futilely at the iron handle did I notice the aluminium sign pointing me round to the back of the building. I was making a hash of this.

I hunched my head as far down into my shoulders as it would go and half-ran round the side. Oh, *this* was Brodie's office. An extension had been built out from the rear of the house and God knew why I hadn't noticed it before, because I swear it was bigger than the original building. It was all sandstone and gleaming slate and glass, with frosted lettering repeating CUMNOCK PROPERTIES GLASSFORD LIMITED in a much more understated font size. The door panels slid smoothly aside with the barest whisper as I walked hesitantly towards them. The woman on reception had raised her head and her eyebrows before I even crossed the threshold.

"Can I help you?"

The official "piss off" of receptionists everywhere. I resisted the urge to go drama-queen and scream "NO-ONE CAN", and shuffled closer to the frosted-glass desk.

"Can I speak to Mr Cumnock." Dear God, I had to stop hanging out with Crow. "Please?"

"Do you have an appointment?" (The backstop 'piss off'.)

I shook my head. She smiled at me.

"Please take a seat."

That had cost her; the sofa along the wall was upholstered in gleaming white leather and I might have showered, but I was under no illusions about the state of my jeans. She must be the consummate professional, though, because she was still smiling as she lifted the phone.

I'll never know how she would have got rid of me, because at that exact moment a pale wooden door swung open and Brodie walked into the reception area. He was talking intently to two other men and a woman, all of them straight from a Commerce & Marketing stock photo library. One man laughed and shook his hand in a businesslike way, the woman nodded to him and smiled, and Brodie winced and frowned and turned his head.

Oh. He'd noticed me. It struck me that I'd timed this *really* badly.

He ignored me until his colleagues had walked out through the magic doors, all three of them shooting me curious and vaguely hostile glances on their way. He watched them walk towards their car, and went on watching for far too long after they'd turned the corner.

Then he swung on his heel, sharp as a sergeant major, and stared at me. "This is unexpected."

I stood up. It seemed respectful. Actually, strike that, it seemed needy to the point of desperation. I said, "I, uh." I brushed at my jeans. "Can I talk to you please?"

"Yes." He folded his arms.

Was that positive? I thought that was positive. I glanced at what I assumed was his office door. The receptionist was poking intently at a tablet screen, pretending she had no idea we were there. Brodie continued to stare at me.

"Can we go into—"

"Not necessary. What did you want to talk about?"

"Ah, the, ah. The bar. Maybe. I wondered if you'd consider maybe I could come back?"

"You mean, do I have any vacancies in your former place of work?"

"Yes." That sounded too curt. "Please." Oh God, now it sounded like begging.

Well, I *was* begging.

He inhaled through his nose, and looked disappointed. He looked me up and down, from my scalp to my trainers.

"Mm-hm. I'd heard you were sorry."

My face felt suddenly like a malfunctioning radiator: no temperature control. I wished more than anything that that receptionist would take her coffee break. I could practically see her ears swivelling.

"Yes," I managed to choke. "I really am."

"I bet you are." He smiled. It wasn't a nice smile.

I wasn't sure if he expected me to say something now. I thought on balance not. And the fact was, I couldn't anyway; all I could do was try to keep breathing.

"You must be joking, Eddie. Right? This is another of your jokes." He took a step to the side and examined me from another angle. "What made you think I'd even consider employing you again?"

It was out before I could stop myself. "Lily said—"

"Lily?" His eyes widened with fury. "My daughter Lily? Are you still trying to see my daughter, Eddie?"

"No, I just—" *What the actual.*

"Good. Because you will *not* be seeing Lily. And you will *not* be working for me. Who'd want you pouring their drink?" His lips looked pale and dry, so he licked them. "Doolan, I wouldn't employ you if you were scrubbing the toilets for nothing. If you were *paying me* to scrub the toilets. Have you got that through your vicious, thick, criminal skull?"

Well, what more was there to say? He wasn't exactly leaving room for negotiation. I nodded. I wanted to leave now. But I couldn't move.

He shifted again, to the other side of me. "You were a good employee, Eddie, I'll give you that. That was what you had going for you, and *it is gone.*"

"Fine," I managed to say. The receptionist was watching me openly now. I caught her eyes, and my stomach lurched: she looked sorry for me. I looked sharply back at Brodie, and it got worse, because along with the disgust there was pity in his stare, too.

"I'm sorry, Eddie, but you're poison now. You're vermin. Nobody likes to see vermin on a night out." He flicked his fingers. "You can go any time now."

It was as if he actually had given my muscles permission. I turned round and walked out through the whispering doors, and kept walking. I walked through the car park and past the bus stop and I kept walking.

Lily had come to my rescue after the train incident, but Lily was never coming to my rescue again. It was like my Walk of Shame had been nothing but a suspended sentence, and all appeals had failed, and it was time for penance.

I walked the fourteen miles home to Langburn.

*

Everything hurt, except the bit that should have, because my heart was like a stone. I pulled off my old trainers and my cheap socks and tentatively flexed my bloody toes. Jesus Gerard Butler gave me no sympathy, but Marv licked a burst blister and seemed to like it. Marv liked everything about me, including my suppurating wounds. I liked Marv.

I liked Sid, too, but I wished she wouldn't keep trying to help me. It was making her look as if she had too much time on her hands.

"Eddie." Behind me, the girl had actually started to rub my shoulders. I should never have let her in. "Don't listen to Brodie. He's a bastard."

"He's a very rich bastard and he owns everything in town and he spawned the girl I love. And he thinks I'm vermin."

"I've said it before and I'll say it again. You're a colossal git but you're not vermin."

"Thank you. Got any local businesses in your portfolio?"

"*Well.* Now that you mention it…"

"Stop it, Sid." I sighed.

"I mean, not me, obviously." Her fingers stopped kneading my neck muscles. "But the good news is, the new BurgerMaster on the Langburn bypass is open. And they're hiring. And I know for a fact Brodie Cumnock doesn't own BurgerMaster. And they probably won't know who you are. Probably. And you get free food if you work there." She peeked over my shoulder to give me her best smile, the one she honestly believed was charming. "The shower's upstairs, first door on the left."

Gillian Philip

16

I hated my jaunty cap, I hated my polyester shirt, and I hated my forced smile. I hated the customers and the way they treated you like you didn't even exist. I hated the drive-thru and the way they spelled it. I hated the bloody burgers.

So as for Sid's vaunted free meals, I never finished any of them. You live with that burger smell all day, you don't really feel like eating the source of it. Anyway, I still wasn't that hungry. I lived chiefly on fries and milkshakes for several days, and when I got desperate I even nicked some dill pickles. But burgers I thought I would never face again, and I could never wash the fat out of my hair.

But hey, I had a cash flow again. It flowed out as fast as it ran in, but at least I could fulfil Marv's enormous capacity for luxury canned chicken. I could walk to work from the bus stop—and a mile in the fresh air never felt so good—and for the next three weeks I did not see a single familiar face. Who'd drive out to the bypass when there was a perfectly good McDonalds in town?

All right, it could never have lasted, but those twenty-two days, after the last few weeks I'd had, were like nirvana. I could hate myself in an atmosphere of steamy, fatty serenity. Jack Michie seemed to have exited my life, without regrets, stage-right in pursuit of a coke-snorting soap star. Twitter had moved on to a cabinet minister's massive class-based gaffe and a simmering war in a country I'd only barely heard of. While I never hoped the peace and quiet would last forever, I knew I was safe till the trial date and (presumably) the sentencing brought it all back up again.

For three weeks, that is.

I didn't even see the group come into the restaurant. I was standing at the counter in my usual state of transcendental meditation, wearing my inane smile and fantasising about mass murder while I took orders. This isn't nearly as sinister as it sounds. Fantasy murder is like a video game: it gets it out of your system. I can't tell you how often I've disembowelled Aoife Connor in my heart, but she's still walking around in perfect health.

"What can I get you?" I asked the newest vague customer-shape, through my smiling teeth.

"I don't believe it," said a voice. The voice was all grin and snicker, and it was doubly disconcerting because I'd just been shooting its owner in the head. In my head. If you see what I mean.

I could only stare at Drew Hunter. Horror roiled in my stomach like a two-day-old burger. God knew what my face looked like, but I was going to know very soon, because Drew whipped out his phone and took a picture before I'd even drawn breath.

The BurgerMaster manager was eyeing me sideways, and frowning in perplexity at Drew and his laughing mates, but I couldn't turn to smile reassuringly at him. I couldn't believe my nemesis was in here, and yet I'd known it was only a matter of time. I knew I'd known it.

"Nice hat," grinned Owen Gregor, leaning forward to flick its peak.

"I am so posting this on Instagram," smirked Mackenzie. He was thumbing his phone as he spoke, and he'd clearly got over the awkwardness of having once been my best mate. He didn't even look shamefaced any more.

"See you finally found your natural level, Doolan," said Drew Hunter. He wasn't smiling, not any more, but his eyes just glowed with triumph and moral superiority.

"Is there a problem here?" said the manager behind my shoulder.

"No," I gritted through clenched teeth.

Mackenzie turned his phone to me so I could see his screen. There I was in full digital colour, looking gormless on his Instagram. GREASY SPOON!!!!!!!!!

Two likes and a LOL already. Why didn't anybody in Langburn or Glassford have a life?

"Chicken burger," said Drew. He stared hard at me, lips twitching. "Medium fries."

I clenched and unclenched my fists. I didn't even want to turn my back on them to get their order.

"Jesus," said Owen. "Talk about promoting somebody beyond their capabilities."

"Ah, leave him alone, Owen." Drew flicked a piece of imaginary dust off my shirt, so viciously he stung my nipple. "He's doing his best. It's just his best doesn't stretch to flipping a burger."

"I'll film it for you, Eddie," said Mackenzie helpfully, lifting his phone again. "So you can watch it back in slo-mo, and see where you're going wrong. YouTube, ya tube. Give it ten minutes to upload. I mean, it'll take you that long to get us the order."

They all laughed.

"Come on, Edmund, give us a smile. You're going viral again!"

"Is it time for your break yet, Eddie?" said the manager. "I can take over here."

He was trying to help me out, I knew he was, but he'd waited just half a second too long. I smiled back at Mackenzie. I joined in the laughter. I struck out and snatched his phone off him, and chucked it in the deep fat fryer.

"Bugger," I said as the three of them stopped laughing simultaneously. "That was an accident."

"Eddie!" barked the manager in horror.

He was saying something else now, but I couldn't hear him. Mackenzie was yelling obscenities at me, lunging across the counter, and Drew and Owen joined in. People were standing up at their tables, peering across. Some of them were hustling their children out the door, shoving their half-finished Playtime Combos into their hands, and some of the kids were starting to wail.

I didn't wait to get fired. I whipped off my cap, chucked it in the fryer after the phone, and walked out.

17

I sat on the back steps and smoked. There was the very first hint of a chill in the air—I could tell from the gooseflesh on my bare arms—but I wasn't bothered. It kept the bottle of Lidl vodka fairly cool, and besides, it was bliss to feel the stink of burgers evaporating off my skin. I wanted everything to evaporate off me. If I could scrub myself down to naked flesh and start again, I would. And this was a start: a cold moon and an empty sky and the vodka and fags stripping my throat lining.

I picked up my phone and checked Twitter while my battery lasted. The photo had been public for three days now, and it had been quickly shared to Twitter, and it was still getting a *lot* of retweets. Another ghost. The haunting, taunting ghost of Mackenzie's phone.

LOL LOL LOL

I was going to have to ration the fags. It wasn't like I could afford to chain smoke.

The battery crapped out. Thank God. I don't know why I still checked Twitter in the first place. Masochist.

I hoped Mackenzie had had no end of trouble editing me out of all his Facebook photos. I hoped he'd had to sweat over Photoshop to do the job properly. I hoped he'd had to buy a special version. I hoped it had taken his bank account into overdraft and they'd slapped him with a twenty-five pound charge. I could have continued this chain of imagined disasters for Mackenzie; but enough with the mimsy vague hostility. I hoped he was going to die messily, slowly and soon.

I set the dead phone down at my side, grateful for a battery life that set limits on me tormenting myself. I had to do something. Anything. My meagre savings were long gone and I'd finally had to give in and sign on. But I didn't want to end up like Crow's dad, fat and malevolent as Jabba the Hutt. I wondered how Crow was, but I didn't have the energy to go round and find out.

Beside me, I felt Marv stiffen, and when I glanced down at him his tail was all puffed out. He jumped up to a nervous crouch, and I smelt his pee.

"You jelly-belly," I said. "There's nothing there." All the same, I reached back and cracked open the catflap, and he shot through it and vanished.

I let it fall shut again, and leaned back on my elbows. I should leave. I should get a train ticket and get the hell out of Dodge. I didn't have anywhere to go, so it would be awkward taking Marv with me, but I could manage. He could tolerate a pet carrier for days at a time, or he could learn to. It should be do-able. I could start thinking about it, at least.

Except there was Crow. I couldn't really leave Crow. Maybe.

And Lily. There was always Lily. But *you will not be seeing Lily.*

I sighed. I felt like I'd been immobilised. Tasered by circumstance. Still twitching, though.

Something moved in the overgrown bushes at the bottom of the garden. I narrowed my eyes and stubbed out my cigarette.

A shape slunk out of the undergrowth, and froze. I went still. Eyes glowed eerily, and finally in the scraps of light spilling out of the house, I made out the shape.

Oh, that was what had spooked Marv. A big dog fox. He paused with one long foreleg raised. His whiskers twitched and his ears flicked forward.

I raised my bottle to him in a toast. In between vanity-searches for my own name, I'd read in the papers that a fox had got number 44's pet rabbit.

He eyed me for a moment longer, then hunched himself low and slinky, flicked his brush and flowed back into the darkness as if he was made of water.

"You should go to bed, Eddie." Sid's voice broke the lovely quietness. She'd probably scared off the fox.

I turned to watch her as she clambered over the fence. "So should you. It's a bit late for stalking me."

"I've been thinking. About you. I did ring the doorbell."

"I disconnected it. I always hated that fucker."

She sat down beside me on the step. "Eddie, do you have to stay here?"

"You want me to go inside the house, or emigrate?"

Sid looked exasperated. "I think you need some space. That's all. You're holed up here and you're scared to stick your nose out in case the neighbours look at you funny, and you spend your whole time just reading about yourself and hating people."

I didn't deny it. "And frying bacon for that scrote next door."

"And feeding Crow, yes. When did you last feed yourself, eh? But apart from that." She took a deep breath. "Change of scene, that's all I'm saying. Can't you get away? Till the trial?"

I lay back again, the edge of the doorstep cutting into my spine, and stared at the moon. "I thought I could try and fix the car. Get away for a bit. Could park up in the middle of nowhere and sleep in it. Where nobody could see the—what's written on it."

"Well, why don't you? It's not the worst idea in the world. You might even be able to respray—"

"My thoughts exactly. I went and looked at the car the other day. Day after I chucked the BurgerMaster job."

"And?"

I rolled my head to face her, and smiled. "I left one of the back windows open a crack. Last time I parked it. Somebody poured in a pint of milk, must've been weeks ago. I can't sleep in it. A destitute refugee couldn't sleep in it. It smells like vomit."

"Oh, Eddie. Oh shit."

"No: vomit. So it could've been worse, right?"

Sid picked up my pack of cigarettes and turned it over in her hands. "I still think you need to go away somewhere. I couldn't stop thinking about it tonight. That's why I came over."

"I can't afford a holiday. And I'm not Brodie Cumnock, Sid, I don't *have* a second home."

"No," she said, "but I do." She smirked, moonlight sparking off her braces.

"No," I said patiently, "you don't."

"Do too."

I stared at her, my mind not whirling exactly; more stumbling out of the murk. "Oh," I said. "The trailer."

"It's a *caravan*."

It was a trailer. I'd seen it.

In fact I'd stayed over sometimes, a few months ago, when we were all young and carefree and went in for barbecues and all-nighters on the beach. Lily was never allowed to stay the night, but a snog in the dunes was better than nothing. My ribcage constricted as I remembered those times. I realised I was old enough to be nostalgic—at nineteen, for heaven's sake—and in my memory the caravan-trailer was a misty place of midnight enchantment, with campfires above the tideline and probably some twat with a guitar, and it smelled of hamburgers in the right way. I licked my lips.

"Aren't your parents using it?"

"Dad's working weekends for the next month. So, no."

I looked for another excuse. "What about Marv? He can't feed himself."

"I'll get him over to my house," said Sid. "He's over there half the time anyway."

Oh, was he? Treacherous little sod.

"Go on," said Sid. "I won't tell anybody where you are. Then at least you won't have to deal with journalists. You'll probably have to tell the police where you are, mind."

"I should think," I said venomously, "that's a sure way of letting the press know, too."

"All the same," said Sid, "you should tell them."

"Yes," I said. "I should."

"And the press can't hassle you at the moment. You know that."

"Yeah," I said. "I did notice I'm not fashionable any more. Except on Twitter, intermittently."

"There isn't any wifi at the caravan," Sid told me persuasively.

"There is that," I mumbled.

"I'll look after Flo," said Sid. "As well as Marv."

"Thanks," I said, "but I haven't said I'm going yet."

Sid smiled her metal smile. "I'll get the key."

18

Of course, Crow turned up in time to take my Xbox before I left. The little sod didn't even ask nicely.

"I know somebody who can fix it," he said. "They've got an old Xbox and they can take the disc drive out and put it in yours. Give it to me."

"For God's sake," I grunted, even as I yanked out the plug and wrapped it round the dead console, "I'm not leaving the country. I haven't got a terminal disease. You're not getting it *forever.*"

"Yeah but can I have it while you're away."

"Punctuation, Crow, *punctuation.*" I shoved the Xbox into his greedy waiting arms. Remembering I felt extra-sorry for him at the moment, I slapped Grand Theft Auto V on top of it.

I had to catch the bus, and even after that it was a two-mile walk to the village where the caravan lived. Still, my backpack wasn't that heavy and at least it wasn't raining. In fact it was swelteringly hot again; not a cloud in the sky. The backpack was stuck to my t-shirt, which in turn was glued to my back, so when I passed the village store I bought a six-pack of beer from the cooler, and chugged one bottle while I waited to pay at the counter. I also bought an all-day-breakfast sandwich, but that was only out of deference to the absent Sid. I chucked most of it in a bin after a couple of hundred metres.

Sid's trailer was at the furthest end of the caravan park, which was at the furthest end of the little village, which was at the furthest end of a long single track road. Her parents had gone for the cheapest site in a park that wasn't terribly popular anyway, so although, as I feared, there were a few holidaymakers frying their skins in deck chairs, and an unreasonable number of kids playing football, Sid's trailer was a little backwater of peace.

It sat in a slight cul-de-sac, huddled with only two other caravans that were shut up and silent, their frilly curtains closed. There was a lump of grassy dune right behind Sid's trailer, and beyond that a more or less deserted beach. The trailer itself had a dilapidated look that appealed to my current frame of mind. And of course, there was the nostalgia factor. It had a dent in its metal flank, and a smear of red paint where I'd once misparked the Vauxhall.

I ran my finger along the paint scrape, amazed to find tiny flakes of red sticking to my skin. In my gloomily fanciful frame of mind, it seemed like a car ghost. Maybe that was how ghosts worked: leaving traces of unexpected dust that made memories spark and flare in your head. Certainly I had a sudden, vivid rerun of that evening in my mind.

I'd only steered so badly because I was having a fight with Lily. She'd been huddled into the passenger seat, unable to cry because she was so furious. Mouth tight, eyes red and blazing, her arms wrapped round herself so tightly they practically made the seatbelt superfluous.

"She can't talk to me like that, Eddie. You *can't let her.*"

"Hello, Earth calling Lily? I *didn't?*"

"I've tried to be nice to her!"

"Well, to be fair, she's tried to be—"

"*No she hasn't!* Hardly ever! Only when you're in the room! Did I tell you what she said to me when you went out of the kitchen the other day?"

"Yes. It doesn't matter—"

"It *doesn't matter?*" She hit my arm hard enough to leave a bruise.

"No, it doesn't matter because she didn't mean it. And she's *not going to do it again.*"

Of course Flo had learned her lesson (she always did). She'd never meant to hurt Lily's feelings, I was sure of it; Flo just couldn't control her tongue sometimes and she was protective of me to a fault. She must have been riddled with guilt, because that was the night she took the gin-and-Xanax cocktail, while I was at the caravan with my friends and with Lily. After that I was confident things would get better for everybody concerned.

Anyway, that was all irrelevant now. Flo was dead, and Lily, according to her father, was dead to me. Or the other way round; whichever way it works.

I unlocked the caravan and made myself at home. As soon as I stepped into the big living area and pulled open the lacy curtains, I felt a fuzzy glow of familiarity. The upholstery of the bolted-down sofas was all nineteen-eighties geometrics in shades of red and grey (though the caravan couldn't have been *that* old), and I remembered the design with fondness. I remembered cuddling up to Lily on those rigid cushions, drinking beer and watching the old television, which had since been replaced with a new small flatscreen. The signal was still intermittent, I realised as I turned on a badly-pixellated version of Channel Four Racing. I switched it off again, and started unpacking.

I hadn't brought much. Most of the space in my backpack was taken up with Flo's rolled-up housecoat; I tugged it out and threw it onto the sofa. I'd brought a t-shirt and a hoodie but no spare jeans. The change of underpants was mostly for Sid's benefit; she'd insisted. Glancing out of the window at the laundry whirligig, I noticed that I needn't have bothered: a pair of Y-fronts drooped on its wires. Sid's dad must have left them on his last visit.

Maybe it was the sea air, but I was starting to wish I hadn't thrown away the remains of my sandwich. If I wasn't careful, Sid would be bringing me roadkill to fatten me up. All the same, I couldn't be bothered walking back to the shop in the village, not right now, so to take my mind off my stomach I went through to the cramped bedroom, pulled the duvet over myself and shut my eyes. I didn't even bother kicking off my shoes.

I'd have sworn I could still smell Lily on the polyester sheets. Ridiculous, after all this time, but maybe that was why I couldn't sleep. I was too hot, and I was too cold, and my brain shimmied inside my skull, buzzing and racing and fluttering like my heartbeat. I was hungry. I was tired. I wasn't tired enough. I hated having time to think.

I threw off the duvet, getting a little shock of static electricity from its cover. As I sat up my phone buzzed, but by the time I answered it the signal had gone. I swore, and stuffed it back in my pocket.

Maybe the beach wasn't the sensible place to go, given its innocent happy memories, but I honestly couldn't think of anything better to do. The little unofficial track that had been beaten through the gorse on the dune was almost overgrown with disuse, but I hacked my way through it with a bit of ornamental driftwood I nicked off the next caravan's doorstep. I emerged at the dune's crest into a brisk but warm easterly wind that tugged at my hair and clothes.

I blinked and chucked the driftwood stick aside. The tide was far out, leaving acres of sand exposed and gleaming in the fierce sunlight. Gulls rode the air currents, a dog barked dementedly as it chased them into the waves, and its owner shrieked and dashed in pursuit. Some middle-aged women scurried in and out of the freezing sea; a bunch of kids in wetsuits basked in it, and laughed at the women. There were people around, then, but it was hardly Torremolinos. I doubted anyone would take the time to look at me, let alone recognise me. Even in my paranoia I realised that.

For the first time in days I felt my heartbeat start to calm. I sucked in a few deep breaths of the salty air. Maybe this hadn't been a bad idea of Sid's after all. I found myself a sheltered nook in the dunes, sat down and took out my cigarettes. And my phone, but when I checked the little bars at the top of the screen, the signal hadn't come back.

No wifi, no phone signal. I liked it here more and more.

I lay back, feeling my back leach warmth into the dry cool sand. But the sun beat down steadily on my front and I wasn't cold. The breeze was blowing sand into my eyes, so I closed them.

And then I fell asleep.

*

"I thought I'd find you here."

The chirpy voice yanked me out of deep, silent blackness, and so fast and brutally that I almost wanted to throw up. God, I must have been more tired than I thought. I blinked, and held my head on to my neck, and waited for the horizon to stop swaying.

"Sid, you didn't think, you *knew.*" I managed to glare at her. "It was you that gave me the key."

"I don't mean the caravan, I mean the beach. This dune. I looked for you at the caravan and then I came here. Were you asleep?"

"Yes, Sid. Yes, I was asleep."

"Sorry. So, what do you fancy doing this afternoon?"

I sucked my teeth, holding onto my patience. *Sleeping,* I wanted to say. *I really quite fancy sleeping some more.* But I already knew I wouldn't drift off again. I staggered to my feet, swiping sand off my backside. Sid waded up the dune and brushed sand off the bits of my back I couldn't reach. Over-familiar, much?

"I tried to phone you," she said, "but the signal's always rubbish here."

"That was part of the point of coming," I told her, with strained patience.

"Yeah, I know. Do you want to go for a walk? Or have a swim? Or do you want to go up to the woods and shoot rabbits?"

"I don't need a chaperone, Sid, and I don't need a nurse. I'm fine, honest."

"Don't lie to me, Edmund."

"Don't *ever* call me Edmund, Sidonie."

"Fair point." She grinned, metallically. "Shooting rabbits it is, then."

To be honest, I'd been hoping she was going to say that. It's not that I've got anything against rabbits. But they're a pest, they're going to get shot by somebody. And my God, it's cathartic.

"Are you allowed to have your dad's shotgun?" I asked her.

"Well, not strictly, but it's within the guidelines."

"No, Sid. No, it isn't. They're not guidelines."

She gave me one of her Looks, beneath which I withered. "Do you want to come or not?"

"If it's a quiet part of the forest," I said, "I'll go along with the guidelines."

19

It was quiet enough. Even the yells and squeals of the wetsuited kids faded as we made our way inland and deeper into the pines. The hysterical barks of the gull-chasing dog were the last remaining sound, and eventually even that died away. I reckoned that unless we ran into a charity cross-country marathon for the Joanna Ricks Foundation, we were safe enough to start shooting.

Little streaks of grey bolted for cover as we crested a low rise, so I slipped in two cartridges and snapped the shotgun together.

"They're long gone," said Sid, shading her eyes with her hand like a pantomime sailor. The sunlight was gentle and dappled, hardly dazzling.

"There'll be more. Woods are crawling with them." I broke the shotgun again. "Why don't we try not talking?"

She took the hint. I had a feeling she wanted to chat, but I didn't feel like encouraging her, and Sid was surprisingly accommodating of my snottiness today. The sound of echoing gunshots was hardly an unusual one in the country, and nobody came running to investigate, so eventually I relaxed enough to stalk properly. Superimposing Drew Hunter's face on one rabbit, and Aoife Connor's on another, did the trick. Neither was a good look for a rabbit, but they didn't have to live with it for long.

Brodie Cumnock Bunny, of course, scampered his way out of trouble and down a hole.

I picked up Aoife Bunny by the hindlegs, and tried to feel bad about it. She was heavy and limp, her eyes glazed, and what's more I realised quickly that she was a boy rabbit.

"Sorry, Aoife," I said. I wasn't sorry at all.

"Does that feel better?" asked Sid, with a sardonically tilted eyebrow.

I sighed. "Not much."

"This'll make you feel better," she said, handing me Drew Bunny and folding her arms. "One of Brodie's companies has just gone tits-up."

"Oh shut up," I said. "It has not."

"Has too. Only one of them, mind. He's got a lot more pies."

I wound a rubber band round and round the hindlegs of both rabbits till they were tightly conjoined. If I stretched it any more it would snap. I was temporarily unable to speak, not because I was lost for words but because there were way too many of them: I was torn between sparkly, sunshiny delight and the dead crushing hand of reality.

"Is Lily still at Dunstane," I said, infected by Crow's speech patterns again.

"Far as I know." Sid shrugged.

I swung the rabbits at my side, feeling unreasonably angry. "Any more redundancies. Has he sold his house. Has he downgraded his car. Has he sold Lily's Beamer."

She swallowed and shook her head.

"He's not in financial trouble," I said. "No way."

"Oh well," said Sid. "It was a nice thought."

"Oh tut, Sid. Your politics of envy."

"Rubbish. I was just trying to cheer you up."

"Maybe it's a tax scam or something."

"Maybe."

Sid sniffed dismissively. "Anyway, he's just given that massive donation to the Jo Ricks thing. Twenty laid off from Molly's Diner, but the rest of his businesses are fine. So he's fine too, isn't he?"

"Yeah. Brodie Cumnock will always be fine."

And I realised it was true. Recession, depression, or zombie apocalypse, Brodie Cumnock would always be fine. There was no way even fate or the universe could ever get the better of him, because that was how the world of Glassford and Langburn worked. Our little local world worked for Brodie Cumnock. Well, the world except for me. I swung the rabbits so violently, the rubber band snapped; they flew from my grip and crumpled against a tree.

"Bugger."

Sid allowed me a moment of quiet contemplation of my idiocy. Then, as I grabbed them up again, she said, "What are you going to do with those rabbits?"

I stared at them. Made a face. "Fancy some meat that's actually fresh?"

*

"I wonder if Marv would like these?" I leaned back on the caravan steps and eyed the gutted rabbits. I really, really didn't feel like eating them, and that made me feel bad for the rabbits and their wasted lives. Even with the faces they'd been wearing when I shot them.

Sid pulled an instant barbecue out of a plastic bag, and shuffled it noisily to level out the charcoal chunks. Her face was pink and slightly sweaty from the walk to the village store, and she fanned herself as she crouched down to strike a match. She'd volunteered to be the one to stay and clean the rabbits, but I'd felt an existential responsibility towards Aoife and Drew Bunny. They lay there dead at my hand, so I'd better be the one to eviscerate and skin them.

And now I was even less inclined to eat them. Because they had big brown eyes and cute noses. If it had *actually* been Aoife and Drew, I might not have felt so bad about it.

Sid tossed aside the shopping bag, and it blustered and bounced away till the breeze pinned it against a gorse bush. "Marv, she said, "would not know what to do with a rabbit. All he eats is canned food. The expensive stuff."

"Yeah," I said. "Sorry about that. He's high maintenance, is Marv. I'll give you more cash."

"Don't bother. You can owe me, gorgeous." She fluttered her unflutterable lashes, and I laughed. The laugh sounded weirdly out of place, and brought me up short. But Sid grinned.

"How is he, anyway?" I asked.

"Eddie, you've only been gone one afternoon. Marvin's fine."

"He eats three times a day," I reminded her.

"You don't know how wrong you are," she said. "He eats at *your* house three times a day."

"Oh," I said glumly. "Well, at least he's used to crossing the road."

"He'll have to be. Mum won't let him stay in the house. Because, er..."

"The incontinence thing," I guessed.

"Uh-huh. I had to scrub the sofa myself, and that was only one visit. But he *will* get fed. Don't worry."

"Well, thanks."

"Do I have to feed Crow as well?"

"God, no." She'd nearly made me laugh again. "Seriously, keep a note of how much I owe you. I'll pay you when I can." I started to take out my cigarettes, then shoved them back when I realised how undiplomatic that would be. Benson & Hedges were more expensive than even Marv's cat food brand.

The coals were glowing grey, so I flipped a couple of ragged bits of rabbit onto the barbecue, the flare of heat singeing my face.

"Well," I said, "look out for him. There's a fox around that he's scared of. And he hates cars. I'm pretty sure there's large hamsters that make him nervous."

"I'll look out for him." Sid patted my arm with hot barbecue tongs, making me wince. "Just relax and try to forget... stuff. Nothing's going to happen to Marv on my watch. Now, dear." She winked. "Leg or breast?"

20

Sid left me the gun.

Sid, you might think, was nearly as far out of her senses as I was, doing such a thing, but Sid knew me better than anybody, now that Flo was a permanent resident of the Burnside Cemetery. Sid knew I would no more stick that gun in my mouth and pull the trigger than I would win Langburn Citizen of the Year. Sid also knew, because I told her quite forcefully, that I would never eat a burger again as long as I lived; and besides, Sid was evangelical about hunter-gathering. There was nothing more heart-healthy and nourishing than a nice lean rabbit; I was doing the local farmers a favour; and Sid knew my opinion on pot-roasted roadkill. That was one conversion she was never going to make.

I'm a bloke. I *liked* shooting. It made me feel all Stone Age and self-sufficient. And I did like rabbit. And I did not want to live on all-day breakfast sandwiches out of the village shop. And rabbits cost the precise equivalent of one shotgun cartridge each.

Sid leaving the gun with me was a criminal offence, but it's not like I was a model law-abiding citizen, and Sid lived on a parallel planet anyway.

So yes, I was toting an illegal weapon, but I could feed myself if I had to. I had a place to sleep that didn't smell of sour milk and vomit. The sense of having to *do something* faded to a low-grade niggle, just like my guilt had, because after all what was there to do? I'd probably be in prison soon, paying my debt to humanity. At least the food-and-bed situation would be simplified. Maybe I could chib somebody behind bars, so I could stay in prison forever. How hard could it be? How bad could it be?

Nothing could be worse than the facts that chased each other through my head, hour after hour after hour, making it impossible even to read one of Sid's dad's knackered crime thrillers. There was a dead woman at the beginning of all those books, a horribly murdered woman, and I kept seeing Lily's face on them.

It was a quirky side-effect of my obsession, that was all. Because Lily had conspired with her dad, she'd giggled and laughed as she agreed to his plan. *How can we humiliate Eddie Doolan even more? Lily, I've got an idea. This is what you'll tell him...*

I was sure of it. Sure of it. Every third time I thought about it, I was sure of it. The other two times I would tell myself: *How can you think that? How can you believe she'd do that to you?*

I couldn't read. I couldn't sleep. I couldn't eat. I shot quantities of adorable big-eyed rabbits that I never ate. I chucked most of them over the fence.

For three days I had the same routine: I went shooting at dawn. I watched a pixellated television screen for five minutes, then gave up. I lay on my narrow bed, smoking. I stubbed one out and lit the next and hated Brodie and Lily and Mrs Slater and Megan the Dozy Barmaid and Mackenzie Clark and Jack Michie and the world.

And then I'd shut my eyes and rest my fag on the ashtray on the duvet, half-wondering if I'd fall asleep and burn myself alive.

*

I started awake, smelling smouldering polyester, and beat it into submission with my trainer. There was a lovely irregular cigarette burn on the duvet cover, but it wasn't exactly Egyptian cotton. I'd buy Sid's mum a new duvet set at Argos.

Well, if I ever had enough left from my Jobseeker's Allowance, I'd buy her one.

My back hurt from the rigid little bed, and from not having room to toss and turn properly. I stood up, feeling fifty years older. I couldn't be bothered emptying the ashtray, so I stuck it on a shelf above the bed and fetched a saucer from the tiny kitchen. I lit another cigarette. I cracked another bottle of supermarket value-brand beer.

I still wasn't hungry.

A purring growl disturbed me. It grew louder far too fast. I sat up sharply on the edge of the bed.

The car was turning into my little private cul-de-sac of three caravans. *No*, I thought. I didn't want a next-door neighbour. Oh *God* and I'd thrown away their ornamental driftwood. I just wasn't capable of *not* getting into trouble.

I pulled on Flo's housecoat, dashed through to the sitting room and peeked out through a crack in the net curtains. The car was pulling up right next to my caravan. I panted out a sigh of relief, but simultaneously gasped, which, being impossible, set me off in a coughing fit. I was still bent double, trying to recover, when there was a rhythmic little knock on the patterned-glass door.

If I hadn't recognised her white BMW, I'd have recognised her distorted shape. I just had the time and coordination to tear off the flowery housecoat. When I dragged open the door, still coughing like a bronchial navvy, Lily stood there haloed in sunlight like an angel.

The universe hated me.

"Eddie!" The angel nearly took a step back, but managed to recover her composure. I noticed she was trying not to inhale too deeply as she stepped hesitantly inside.

"Hi, Lily," I wheezed.

"You've been smoking a lot." She shut one eye and wrinkled her nose, adorably.

And thank God I have, I couldn't help thinking. At least the tobacco fug covered up the smell of me, to an extent. "I've been kinda bored," I said lamely. "'Scuse me a minute. Have a coffee."

I hurried to the squashed shower room. I didn't have time to shave or have a long, necessary shower, but the least I could do was brush my teeth. I did it for at least two minutes.

When I returned, Lily was filling the kettle and spooning coffee into mugs. Unlike Sid, she hadn't instantly started cleaning up after me. I had to respect that. I felt the heat of shame flood into my face as I stared around the kitchen. Listlessly I picked up an empty beer bottle and dumped it in the bin. It was as much effort as I was willing to make, but it was a start. That and the toothbrush.

"How'd you know where I was?" I asked.

"Sid told me." Lily wouldn't quite meet my eyes.

Thanks for that, Sid. I didn't know if I meant it or not.

Lily poured boiling water into the mugs. She opened the fridge, discovered there wasn't any milk, and shut it again. She stirred the two coffees. For quite a long time.

"I burned a hole in the duvet cover," I said, by way of saying something. Anything.

"Eddie-I'm-really-sorry," she blurted.

I couldn't help making a face. "It wasn't expensive or anything."

She turned to me, a mug in each hand. She slammed one down beside me, making it slop onto the counter. She didn't wipe it up and neither did I. She looked as if she was about to burst into tears. "I mean I'm sorry. I'm sorry I didn't call you after you went to see Dad."

"I, uh…"

"He told me exactly what happened. What he said to you. And I was so embarrassed, but I should've called. I'm really sorry." She put down the other coffee mug and squeezed her hands together. "I meant to call you or text you or something but it was really hard."

"Please stop saying you're sorry," I said. "You're making me nervous."

"Sorry."

I looked at the worn carpet. It was filthy. I didn't think it had been like that when I arrived.

"My dad said I wasn't to see you again," said Lily.

"I know he did." There was hot sharp hatred in my gullet.

"I honestly thought he'd listen to you. I wanted to speak to you but he confiscated my phone," said Lily on a gasp of misery. "I only got it back last week, and then I thought you'd be so mad at me I wanted to come and see you in person. But I had to wait till Dad was busy and then I couldn't find you."

"I was kind of hiding," I said, feeling terrible.

"I know," said Lily, and lunged for me.

That was the most awkward kiss in forever. She was all hesitant, possibly because she was worried I wouldn't reciprocate, but more likely because of the state of my bodily hygiene. I was all self-conscious because I was fully aware of the latter. I could barely spare the focus to be aroused. I was too busy worrying that despite the two-minute scrub, her tongue would find a scrap of rabbit in my teeth.

She drew away from me, blinking, and breathing reassuringly fast. I, on the other hand, was numb. I was always numb now.

Looking slightly confused, she picked up her coffee and sipped at it, rhythmically. I followed suit.

That had not been my finest hour. I cleared my throat.

"I really missed you, Eddie," she said.

"Uh, yeah, Imissedyoutoo," I rushed out. "Sorry, Lily. I'm a bit… thrown. Confused. Is all." Belatedly, I felt my heart creak and groan back into a semblance of a beat. It ached. As did my groin.

"Don't give up on me, Eddie." She looked at me very intently.

"Course I won't," I said. I wanted very much to take her hand, so it was more than a relief when she reached out for mine.

Since I'd been given a prompt, I kissed her again. That one worked better. It worked so well that in the end, it was Lily who had to pull away, and she only did that when her phone buzzed between us.

"Oh, shit," she said, peering at the screen. "It's my dad."

A tingle scurried up my spine. Not a nice one. "Does he know where you are?"

She shook her head. "Wouldn't put it past him to track my phone."

"You're joking, right?"

"Of course I'm joking." She gave me a wry smile. "But I'd better go."

Oh God, do you have to? I'd almost forgotten how much I liked her. But now I remembered, and I desperately didn't want her to go. I didn't want to be left alone again in this bloody little caravan, the one that was sleazy and filthy and smelly because I'd made it that way. If Lily went I'd only get worse, I knew I would. *Please stay please stay please stay.*

"Yeah," I said. "I suppose you'd better go."

"I'll come back. I'll come and see you as soon as I can."

"Yes. Do."

"Take care of yourself, Eddie."

"Okay," I lied.

She kissed me again. I kissed her back again. *Don't leave me here. Don't go.*

She left. She backed out of the door, still kissing me. It was me who had to close it in the end, as her car purred away and disappeared round the corner of the cul-de-sac.

I leaned against the door. What was wrong with that girl? Couldn't she read my mind or something?

Did Lily *ever* bother reading *anybody* else's mind?

Flo always said Lily was self-obsessed.

I don't think she's the girl for you, Eddie. She only thinks of herself. Not you.

Does Lily pay you any attention, Eddie? When was the last time she phoned you?

You ask me, that Cumnock girl's spoilt.

Why would I listen to a word of that? I loved Lily. Flo didn't know her, not really. Flo didn't understand about Lily's strict private school and her possessive father and her obligations to music lessons and Debate Soc and after-school drama class. Lily had a lot to fit into her life, and Flo refused to understand that I didn't *mind* being Fitted In.

I was beginning to wonder, though. I mean, I was lucky to be Fitted In at all, at this point in my life, but the jab of resentment was a sort of involuntary spasm. The horrible notion snaked into my head: *maybe Flo was right about Lily all along.*

Flo was often right, about an awful lot of things.

Hell, no wonder Flo got frustrated with me. Sometimes it was all she could do to cope. Sometimes she barely coped at all. I could drive a nan to drink.

I stood there in the caravan's stinking kitchen, clenching my fists so hard my nails were drawing blood from my palms (yep, my nails hadn't been cut in a while either). I didn't want to stand here like a moron, but I didn't want to go back to bed and I certainly didn't want to drink Lily's godawful coffee, which was cold anyway. I had no idea which way to move.

So thank God for Sid, who walked in without knocking. Thank *God* for Sid. I was so relieved to see her I almost cried.

"Eddie *Doolan*," she said, and stared at me in horror.

At which point I actually did cry.

*

"How's Marv?" I croaked.

We lay side-by-side on the bed, staring at the ceiling. I was smoking (again); Sid lay with her hands demurely crossed. She'd stopped hugging me when I finally stopped blubbing, and now we were in that very awkward post-blub moment when you're both trying to pretend no emotions were actually harmed in the making of this scene.

"Marv's fine," she told the ceiling. "He misses you but he's okay. Spends his life trotting between houses. And eating."

"And peeing on the sofa," I said. "I don't doubt."

"I could lock the cat flap and keep him out of your house."

"No," I said. "Don't do that. Worse things happen to soft upholstery."

She sighed anxiously. "Don't smoke in bed again, Eddie."

I rolled my head round to give her a dry look, and waved my fag in the air. That made her giggle. Which made me giggle. In short order we were both hysterical and helpless. I nearly burned another duvet cover.

Sid wiped her eyes at last. "I'm going to clean this sodding caravan, and don't you dare say a word."

"Yes, miss."

"And you can bloody well help."

"Yes, miss."

We both sighed simultaneously, a juddering joint sigh because we were still recovering.

"I'm also going to bring you some proper food," she said. "Have you seen yourself?"

"Thanks," I said. "I'm not promising to eat it."

"The food I bring, you will eat." She gave me a stern look.

"I'll do a deal with you. Bring me some booze as well, and I'll line my stomach before I drink it."

Sid narrowed her eyes. "All right. Just don't do a Flo."

Of all the girls in all the caravans in all the world, Sid was the only one who could say that to me and get away with it. "I won't," I said meekly.

"I'm serious. It's genetic, you know. Don't overdo it."

"Flo wasn't that bad," I muttered, reaching for my cigarettes. "She was bored, that's all. If she was bored she'd have a drink."

Sid was watching me again. I almost imagined a trace of pity in her face.

"Seriously!" I said. "She wasn't that big a drinker. Most of the time."

"Well." Sid pursed her lips. "Don't get bored, is all."

"Suggestions welcome," I said sarcastically.

"*All* suggestions?" she leered.

I rolled my head sideways on the pillow again, planning to tell her to give it up, for heaven's sake, because it was never going to happen. My nose bumped into Sid's, and I thought I was going to start laughing again, but I didn't. I watched her very close-up, shutting one eye so I wouldn't see double. The nose was just, like, *there*, so I kissed it.

She opened her glinting mouth in surprise and I couldn't stand the curiosity any more. I touched her braces with my tongue, and Sid squeaked, so I kissed her.

At which point, things got a bit out of control.

Gillian Philip

21

Flo wasn't that big a drinker. Most of the time.

If Flo did drink big, the rest of the time, I only had myself to blame. I shouldn't have worried her by coming home late so often. It wasn't like I had a curfew—I was seventeen, for heaven's sake, and she was my nan, not my mother—but Flo had certain expectations, one of which was that I wouldn't drive her out of her mind with worry.

It happened so often I'd stopped treating it as a big deal. If she was capable of standing up, she'd fling herself at me and cuddle me to death, but usually, when I unlocked the door and walked in, she was prone and floppy on the sofa, so all she could do was stare at me and burst into noisy tears of relief.

Flo, I'd say. *Flo, I'm not that late. Am I that late?* I'd look at my phone.

She'd howl. I'd crouch down beside the sofa and put my arms round her with difficulty, and feel terrible.

I didn't know where you were, she'd manage to hiccup.

And I'd try not to flinch from the sweet fumes of gin. *I was just seeing Lily, Flo.* Or, *I was out with my mates, that's all.* Or, *I was at work, remember?*

I forgot, I forgot. Oh Eddie. She'd blow her nose hard into my shirt. *I never seem to see you any more.*

Guilt would squeeze my ribcage. *I'm sorry, Flo.*

Oh no, Eddie, don't mind me, you've got to have young company. She'd blow her red raw nose again, and wipe her red raw eyes. There was always mascara all over the place. *I was so worried, I thought you'd left me, I thought you didn't love me any more.*

Bloody hell, Flo. Of course I love you, I'd mumble, mortified.

I love you too, Eddie. You won't leave me alone. I know you won't. Sometimes she'd get a new lease of energy then, and she'd practically leap off the sofa to wrap her arms round my neck, enfolding me in her Victoria-Beckham-and-gin aura.

I'll stay home tomorrow night.

Will you? Oh Eddie. You're such a good lad. I don't know what I'd do without you. I just don't know what I'd do.

And what can you say when somebody loves you that much? What could I do but cancel umpteen dates with Lily, countless evenings with the lads? Easier to make Flo happy, frankly, and less grating on the conscience.

I wouldn't have Flo around forever. She was in her late sixties, for God's sake. And looking back now I was glad I'd given her the attention. There'd be other evenings. There'd even be other girlfriends. You didn't get spare nans.

Flo loved me more than life itself. Even if they don't set a price on it, you owe a person who loves you like that. And given what happened to her, I'm still glad I paid up.

*

Sid wasn't about to make any demands. She seemed allergic to the very notion of expecting anything from me. I wasn't sure whether to be flattered or not.

"Don't worry, I won't stalk you," she smirked as she stowed the tiny hoover in its tiny cupboard, wrapping the suction hose tightly round it. "I know you're on the rebound."

"I am not on the rebound," I muttered half-heartedly. I couldn't be mad at her. The caravan was unrecognisable. Or rather, had you been her caravan-proud parents, it was a lot more recognisable than it had been three hours ago. There was still an underlying whiff of smoke, sweat and bad food, but mostly it smelt of Cif and bleach.

Sid looked smug, and not just about the hoovering. I myself felt a tingly glow that was deeply inappropriate. I should feel worse about being unfaithful to Lily; but I wasn't sure I had been. Were Lily and I still a Thing? I had no idea, but maybe I should have resolved that issue before turning my lust elsewhere.

Out of absolutely nowhere, an unpleasant thought crossed my mind. I thought: at least I never have to cancel a date again. At least my nights are my own these days. At least I don't have to pay regular loving homage to Flo in case she goes back to the pills and booze.

I picked something unidentifiable out of the sink drain with my fingernails, and flicked it into the bin with a shudder.

Forget it, I told myself: You've thought worse things than *Flo's not an issue any more*.

"Hey, what's this?" Sid had opened the caravan door, on her way to emptying the Hoover bag. She peered down at the step, then crouched down to pick something up.

In my still-jangled state of paranoia I half-expected an envelope full of dogshit, so I had to blink a couple of times before I registered it was a neat, flat plastic package. It was a terribly expensive-looking John Lewis duvet set, cream with gold embroidery.

Sid extracted it from its packaging, shook it out and admired the pattern. "Pretty."

I licked my lips. "Shit," I said.

Sid glanced at me. "Uh-oh. You think?"

I didn't think, I knew. Lily *had* been listening to me, she *had* been concerned, she *had* wanted to help. She must have come back while Sid and I were busy, and I'm not talking about the housework. And if Lily hadn't just knocked louder and walked in, it must mean she'd noticed something. Realised something. God, *heard* something.

My stomach twisted.

"Whoa," said Sid, crumpling her handfuls of the beautifully-pressed duvet cover. "This complicates things."

"No it doesn't," I protested. "We're not a Thing any more. Me and Lily." I could hear a shameful whine in my voice.

"I hope *she* knows that." Sid made a face.

Lily's car might be a precision-tuned, purring Beamer, but how had I not heard it arriving? I kind of knew the answer to that one, but I was too mortified to think about it. I was also tormented by the notion that I should be feeling something other than embarrassment.

"You don't think it could have been somebody else?" Sid pulled out a matching pillowcase. She was beginning to look guilty.

"Nobody else would have a brand-new duvet set sitting at home unopened. Hell, nobody knows I'm *here*."

"Well, Crow knows. But he's the only one."

"Oh, does he? Cheers very much. He'd sell my soul for thirty pieces of Haribo."

Sid shrugged lamely. "I didn't actually tell him, he guessed. He worked it out, and I couldn't deny it. I'm a terrible liar."

I knew that. Sid was so blunt she never had to practice fibbing. "Well, I guess your parents are going to want this place back soon anyway." It had only been a few days but the thought of leaving the caravan made my heart blacken and shrivel inside me. I couldn't begin to imagine submitting myself to the stares of the neighbours again, and the silent, appalled disappointment of Mrs Slater at the corner shop. I wondered where Flo had got her Xanax, and what it tasted like mixed with gin.

"I was going to tell you, and I didn't know how. Dad's got the weekend off after all. They're planning to come and stay here." Sid's eyes were huge with apology.

"I'll open the windows and air it. They'll never know I was here. I promise."

"That's not what worries me," said Sid.

Outside there was the crunch of gravel. I started, and twitched aside the net curtain, which made me feel like the neighbours at number 44. I watched a small figure stomp round the side of the caravan, hands in his pockets, mouth working on what I guessed was a sugar-coated sour jelly candy.

"Speak of the treacherous little devil," I said.

22

Crow was another of those types who didn't wait to be invited in. Thank God he hadn't turned up three-and-a-half hours earlier.

He did actually knock, but just the once, and then he marched in anyway and crashed the rattling door behind him. It shivered in its frame.

"Crow," I said, with heavy disapproval.

Heavy or not, the disapproval flew straight over his head. His eyes flickered and roamed round the caravan interior as if he was checking it for loose valuables.

"Hi Eddie. Police are looking for ya."

We were standing in the kitchen, so there wasn't anything to sit on. All I could do was lean hastily back against the cooker, and hope I looked casual.

"Why?" I rasped.

"You were supposed to be in court this morning, you muppet."

I blinked at him, not understanding. I tugged my phone awkwardly out of my pocket, and checked the date. I swore. I swore again.

"Did you not remember the date."

"No, Crow, I did not remember the date!" Panic made bile burn my throat. "Well, I did, but I never knew it was here already!" I stood up straight. I flopped back against the cooker again. I swore again.

"You better go down now."

Sid looked at me nervously. "Yeah, Eddie. You'd better go down."

I rubbed my hands across my face. "I'll go tomorrow."

"I don't think you should wait till—"

"I'm not going now!" I barked. I needed some time. I needed to think. I needed to agonise, because I hadn't done *nearly* enough of that lately.

Anyway, it was after five. Didn't the police close the office at five and go to the pub?

No, I didn't suppose they did, but I'd grab any excuse and hang on. "Did you tell them where I was?" I asked Crow, a little aggressively.

"Course not. I'm not a grass."

Grass? Who did he think I was, Mad Frankie Fraser?

"But they'll work it out, though, won't they."

"I dare say they will, Crow, I dare say they will." I sighed. I was comfortable leaning against the cooker. I didn't think I'd ever move. "Sid, I'll go home tonight."

"You sure?" She bit her lip.

"Yeah." I looked miserably around the caravan. "Might as well go while it's clean. Get my own booze. Get my own food," I added when I saw her face.

"I got your Xbox fixed," said Crow.

He said it like he thought it would cheer me up. Poor old Crow. I thought about my Xbox; I thought about driving round Los Santos in my Lamborghini like I owned the place and everyone in it. I thought about torturing spies and saving cargo ships from terror attacks. I thought about my noble self-sacrifice online at Level Seven and the ultimate victory of my team. I thought about being a hero, and how it used to feel.

"You can keep the sodding Xbox," I said.

He never objected, he never protested. His little eyes shone and he said "Yeah!"

Sid looked at me oddly, but she pressed her lips together and didn't say a word.

"I'll get packed now," I said, finally disengaging my backside from the cooker.

"Are you going to be okay?" said Sid.

I shrugged. "Why wouldn't I be?"

She didn't answer, just started rearranging the cleaning stuff under the sink.

"Is Sid your girlfriend now," said Crow, following me through the caravan to the bedroom.

"No, I—how's that your business?" I snapped, rolling Flo's housecoat into a tight bundle and stuffing it into my backpack.

He glanced knowingly round the room. "Just wondering. Thanks for the Xbox. You still looking for a best mate."

"Crow, I am *never* looking for a best mate."

"Oh well. Shout if you want to borrow the Xbox."

"Thanks a million, Crow, I *really* appreciate that."

"You're welcome." He rubbed his nose on his sleeve, folded his arms and hung around watching me.

Poor little lonely bastard. I should have said he could be my best mate; it wasn't like the position was occupied. I didn't do Best Friends. I hadn't since I was nine, for heaven's sake. I'll tell you how long it had been since I had a best friend: the last one was Drew Hunter.

"Best mates aren't all they're cracked up to be," I told Crow, by way of surly reassurance. "You're only ten. Play the field a bit. Don't settle down. Make them come to you."

He grinned, suddenly and widely. Crow had a disconcertingly endearing grin; it was probably why he got away with so much. Actually, I didn't know why the little sod *didn't* have more pals.

"Do you think you and Drew would still be mates if that thing hadn't happened."

I glared at him. So this was the thanks I got for being nice?

"No," I said. "Drew was always a little shit. Took me a while to notice, that's all."

"I heard he used to be okay." Crow shrugged.

"Drew was never okay," I said. "Even my nan used to tell me that."

"Yeah but your nan didn't like *anybody*."

I straightened. I stared at him. He shrugged again and looked away.

"Well," he grunted. "She's the one that told his dad on him."

"Somebody had to tell his dad," I pointed out acidly. "He was poisoning cats."

"No he wasn't," said Crow. "Remember it wasn't him remember."

"Well, I forgot. I forgot it wasn't him."

"No you never." Crow gazed at me serenely, still chewing. He popped another Tangfastic into his mouth. "You're maybe saying you forgot but you never."

I thought about throttling him, but maybe he was right. I wasn't sure I had forgotten. Maybe I'd just unconsciously added the fictional cat poisonings to my catalogue of grievances against Drew Hunter. After all, to mix a metaphor, one more wouldn't break the bank.

"Your nan said she caught him putting out those poisoned chicks for them and she told his dad and Drew got hell from his dad, but he never did it."

"Somebody was poisoning cats," I said, my hackles rising, "and even if it was mistaken identity, Drew turned out to be a dick anyway."

"Yeah but he wasn't killing cats was he."

"No," I grunted.

Turned out, when timings were belatedly checked, that Drew had a total, watertight alibi, one that his dad had to accept because his dad was, after all, an officer of the law. But the temporary upshot was that Drew got grounded and punished and stopped speaking to me forever (and vice versa). The real culprit never was found, but the poisonings stopped, so at least the cats of Langburn could sleep safe in their fleecy beds at night.

"So your nan shouldn't have accused him should she."

"My nan," I gritted through clenched teeth, "had good instincts." All through primary school I'd considered me and Drew to be inseparable—I'd spent a lot more time with him than I had with Flo––but the cat business had done the trick. Even at the age of nine I'd said some vicious things to Drew about dead cats, and about the kind of people who make them dead. I'd always liked cats. Probably more than I ever really liked Drew.

And Flo had been right anyway. About Drew Hunter. If not about the cats.

"Go home," I said, suddenly unforgiving. "I've got to get packed."

Crow shrugged. He went home.

*

So did Sid. She hugged me, in a slightly more than sisterly way, but she didn't linger and smooch. I was grateful. She put away the last of the cleaning stuff, looked with satisfaction around the gleaming caravan and kissed me a brisk goodbye. I was so confused by the whole day's events, she was gone before I could call her back and remind her about the gun.

Swearing, I pulled it out from the bottom of the compact wardrobe. I broke it, checked it was empty, then stroked its double barrels, paralysed with indecision.

It seemed much more irresponsible to leave it in a vulnerable unoccupied trailer than to take it with me, so I sighed and unclipped the forestock, then disassembled the gun. I wrapped the stock and the forestock in Flo's housecoat and pushed the whole bundle back into my pack, then shoved the double-barrel as well as I could down the back. It just about fitted; it was just about inconspicuous. I put the box of cartridges on top, then arranged my spare t-shirt over the jutting end of the barrel. Given the state of the t-shirt, I didn't think anyone would want to touch it to look underneath. And I was only catching a bus. When I got home, I could take the gun straight round to Sid's.

I stepped back and eyed the pack. Time to go, then. Definitely time to go.

Obviously I was looking for an excuse to delay that, so when the last bottle of beer occurred to me, I sighed in relief, opened the fridge, and took it out to the beach.

I slithered down the side of a dune, found a comfortable position without stones or prickly grasses, and popped the bottle cap. Another calm before another storm. The only thing missing was Marv. The rest of them I could do without. Even Lily.

The sea was dark blue at the horizon, calm and silvery closer to shore; the waves were small and gentle, sucking listlessly at sand and tiny pebbles. The muted rush of it was soothing. A distant motionless tanker was outlined between sea and sky, the back of my neck was warm with sunshine, and the beer was frosty. My heartbeat calmed a little.

I wished that beer could go on forever, but the last mouthful was warm and flat, and just at the moment I drank it, the sun went behind a cloud. Sighing, I stood up and dusted off sand; like a good citizen I even dumped the empty bottle in the recycling bin on my way past. I heard it crash and shatter against the others, just as a car screeched to a halt beside my caravan.

I turned and stared. The door of the blue Mercedes swung open, and Brodie Cumnock stepped out. Slowly I closed the lid of the bottle bank as he strode towards me.

"This is where you're hiding out." He didn't crack a smile.

I couldn't exactly shake my head, and I didn't want to nod in agreement, so all I could do was stand there like an idiot.

"My daughter came here earlier." It wasn't a question.

I licked my lips and opened my mouth.

"I told you I don't want Lily anywhere near you," he said, very quietly. Too quietly.

"I didn't ask her to—"

"Maybe not, Eddie, maybe not. But the fact she felt she could come here means you're not taking this seriously."

I licked my lips again. "How did you know?"

"That she was here? There's an app for that, Eddie. It's called 'Find My Dimwitted Daughter's iPhone.'"

So. Tracked her phone, like she said. And she'd thought she was joking.

He flattened his hair with both hands and gave a patient sigh. "Eddie, when I said you were poison, I didn't say that was my personal opinion. It may well be, don't get me wrong, but that's not what's important here. You're poison in this town. You're toxic to anyone who knows you. That's why I don't want Lily to know you, do you get that? In a way it's not even personal."

"In a way it is," I said.

"Hell, yes. But it's also good business. You know what's bad business? Keeping rats in the kitchen."

His voice was entirely reasonable. But he meant it all, every word. *Vermin, Eddie.*

It didn't really sting at all. I knew it anyway.

"I'm sorry about what happened to you, Eddie. If I looked at it sideways through some kind of reality filter and thought it over for twenty years and read some scientific journals, I might even understand what the flying piss you thought you were doing. But you did it and it's over and it's done. And *you* did it. *You.*"

Something cold and angry stirred inside me. "If you pity me again," I said, staring into each of his eyes in turn, "I will kill you."

He shook his head, unintimidated. He almost smiled. Well, why would he believe me? My word was nothing. My word was like me: it was pure poison piss.

"You know what I don't understand, Eddie? Why you're still here. How can you stay? Why don't you get the hell away from Langburn? That's what I'd do if I was stupid enough to be in your situation. Get the hell away."

"I was trying to," I muttered.

"Not far enough, Eddie, not nearly far enough. Get out of Langburn, because you'll never get a job in a hundred miles of it. Get out of everywhere in reach of Langburn. Fuck off just as far as you can and then just a little bit further, Eddie. It's not just for everyone else; it's for you. Stop being around here. Just stop."

This time I had nothing left. He watched me for a long time, tilting his head as if he expected some kind of comeback, but I wasn't capable of giving it to him.

He shook his head again. I watched him stride back to his Mercedes, rev it like Lewis Hamilton and back out of the cul-de-sac at top speed. It was very wrong of me to hope he'd hit somebody's puppy. And he didn't. Brodie didn't hurt puppies.

The engine noise had faded and he was long gone by the time I'd stopped being numb and was angry enough to punch him in the throat. I clenched my fists, I clenched what felt like every muscle in my body. I realised I was making a snarling sound that sounded odd and alien even to me. I wanted Brodie back, because I wanted to hit him more than I'd ever wanted anything, more than I'd longed to be allowed to love his daughter.

I wanted to kill him, and I couldn't, because the bastard had gone.

Stop.

Just stop.

23

I couldn't go home in daylight. I realised that fairly fast. I couldn't bear it, couldn't stand to show my face, not even on the bus. I stayed in the caravan, crouched in a huddle on the sofa, and I didn't turn any of the lights on. I didn't even turn the television on. I watched the light fade on the vacuumed carpet and the geometric upholstery, and I waited till even the last glow of the twilight sky had died, and God knew that took forever, because it was the height of summer. I don't even know what I thought about, all those hours. I don't think I thought at all.

But the last night bus into town was at half past midnight and I had two miles to walk before I got to the stop on the bypass, so eventually I made myself uncurl and stagger to my feet. I picked up my backpack from its place beside the door; it weighed like forty shotguns, but I struggled into the straps. I locked the caravan. I started to walk.

It wasn't even properly dark yet. Black night didn't really fall at this time of year. It wasn't dark enough to see stars. The sky was a kind of charcoal-navy, blanketed in cloud, and the world was silent. I trudged up the single-track road in a haze, thinking about nothing but the next footfall, and not a single car passed me. I don't think I've ever been so tired in my life—my blood might have been tar, and my brain was a thick wad of padding inside my aching skull—yet one foot kept sluggishly plodding after the other.

I reached the bus stop three minutes before the bus did, and apart from the driver I was the only person on it. He didn't look pleased at having to stop, but I was impervious by now to the sullen glares of strangers. There was that. Maybe I'd finally stopped caring what people thought of me.

Just as well, really.

Three stops before the outskirts of Langburn, I got to my feet, almost without thinking, and pressed the request buzzer. Lurching down from the bus, I stood in the lay-by and watched it chug into the distance till its red lights blinked out round a corner. The quiet of the night, once the bus had gone, seemed even heavier.

Even in almost-darkness, the Burnside Cemetery driveway looked primped and glossy. Clipped cypresses stood at military intervals along the grass verges, and even in shades of grey they looked pretty. It was that kind of cemetery. A new one. No rambling ivy or tilted headstones or illegible inscriptions, no eerie mausoleums; just shining granite and acid-etched pictures of cars and favourite dogs, and neat little clusters of artificial roses in football-team colours.

The entrance pillars, in the daytime, were smooth honey-coloured sandstone; at this hour they were just a different shade of tasteful grey. I pushed open the gate, without a single spooky creak, and walked up the cinder path towards Flo's tombstone. Somewhere in the pines on the ridge an owl hooted, over and over. That at least was properly atmospheric.

I couldn't get to Flo's grave without walking past the other one. And there was no missing it, there really wasn't. It was heaped in fresh bouquets; there were ribbons and teddy bears and a substantial white arrangement that spelled 'MUMMY'. The chrysanthemums on that one had wilted long ago, and their scent was over-sweet and musty, but it hadn't been removed. All the other flowers were fresh, as if they'd been placed only yesterday.

What went through your head, Jo Ricks?
What on earth went through mine?

I skirted the last resting place of PC Joanna Ricks, 28, and walked on till I found Flo's. The owl hooted again as I slung down my backpack and sat down. Somewhere far away, a fox yelped.

The soil had settled quite a bit since I'd last been here. In the fixed urn beneath the headstone Sid had placed fresh carnations that could have been white, pink or yellow. I pulled out my phone and turned on its flashlight. The flowers were pink. I aimed the beam onto the granite and its inscription.

FLORENCE EMILY DOOLAN
'FLO'
MUCH LOVED NAN
MISSED EVERY DAY

It wasn't much, compared to her Facebook page. Really she'd have wanted sunsets, kittens and effusive tributes with a lot of 'likes'. Kittens, though, would have been just too ironic.

The flashlight was violent and dazzling in the darkness of the graveyard, so I turned it off and loaded Flo's Facebook page on my phone screen. The top tribute hadn't changed; no-one had returned to her page since I'd last looked. I scrolled down. And down. I read each post, and scrolled again. I went way, way back, to a time and an online place where Flo was alive; by that time my back was beginning to ache badly. I wriggled round, leaned my back against her headstone and read on, listening to her voice in my head.

Ah, Flo. So many friends in the cybersphere. So loved. So troubled.

She'd had good mates, though. Her oblique cries for sympathy got plenty of attention. *Don't worry, Flo, babe, we love you.*

Some people just don't appreciate you but we do, right guys?

Love ya, Flo, stay strong xxxxxx

There was even an actual *U ok, hon?*

It wasn't that I hadn't read her Facebook page before. Fact is, although we weren't Facebook friends, I'd often clicked over for a read, even when she was alive. Flo's page wasn't private; that wouldn't have been like her. What she didn't know, despite being such a silver surfer, was how transparent her log-in password was, how easy it was to guess. Not her birthday: her retirement date.

I'd hovered many times over her page buttons, tempted to pry further. I'd logged in as Flo several times, my fingers itching, but I'd never actually gone as far as reading her private messages. It wasn't pure nobility; it wasn't about respect, though that's what I told myself at the time. The truth was, I kind of knew what the messages would be like, and I didn't want to read them. Not when she was alive. Certainly not when she was newly dead.

Well, it wouldn't bother her now.

I clicked and linked and scrolled. I sucked in a deep breath, and read on. My back was warm against her headstone, as if she was reaching out and embracing me.

I flicked and flicked with my thumb, taking each message thread back to its beginning as Flo's headstone-ghost snuggled tight against my spine, as if she was reaching out to grab me from a grave that was way too shallow. There was a film of sweat on my back but I couldn't move. At least I couldn't hear her voice in my head; she'd fallen silent now that she was there onscreen. Maybe she was reading over my shoulder.

Lily hadn't poisoned any imaginary cats, like Drew had, but Flo's creative juices were limitless. Lily's crimes were mostly small, but they were many. Putting horse pee in Flo's perfume. Pouring her gin down the sink. Telling Eddie his nan had dementia and she belonged in a home. Gossiping to Flo and laughing about the poor old disabled man at number 36. Anyway, by the time I'd read four message threads, with their increasingly desperate pleas for the world to *see what Lily Cumnock's really like*, I couldn't stand the girl myself.

My nan was clever. Bloody clever. I was almost proud of her.

Because Lily was guilty of none of it. She'd told me what Flo was up to, of course, told me she knew Flo was spreading terrible rumours about her, but I never did take her complaints too seriously. I mean, I should have done. No wonder she hit me and made me bang the Vauxhall into the side of Sid's caravan.

Look, Flo was bored. She didn't have enough to do.

That's why she was a little bit addicted to comment threads. She had opinions, like anybody else. And God, did Flo like to express them.

Anonymously, of course, but I knew all her pseudonyms. I used to see them when I brought her gin and biscuits, when she was typing too frenetically to take a break. I could see her below-the-line opinions over her shoulder and I knew what she was doing but it kept her busy. It gave her an interest in life. It kept her attention away from me.

I clicked desultorily on links to her favourite news sites until the phone beeped at me, faded and blinked off, the battery as dead as Flo.

I didn't have any excuse for tolerating the comment threads, for letting her spew out her sometimes-sugary vitriol. I'd read all of it, I reckon, even at the time. We shared that ancient laptop and I used to search Flo's comments every night by her many usernames, because I thought one day I would do something, I would confront her and stop it happening. I never did, because I didn't want to challenge her. I didn't want to have the conversation. I was a coward. If I didn't even confront her about the dead cats, I was hardly going to question a few clicks on a keyboard.

So in a way they really were my fault, all those abusive tweets and rape threats, the horrible mutilating deaths she promised to columnists and actors and reality TV stars. And all the bullying rants and the hideous insults she threw at everyone from bereaved parents to unfortunate politicians, they were down to me too. It was my fault Flo abused the mother of that murdered toddler, my fault Flo taunted her for leaving the child alone for thirty seconds.

I was partly responsible for it all, because I'd kept my mouth shut and pretended none of it was happening, so maybe it was a kind of poetic justice that the police were about to hold me to account. I deserved to take responsibility. I just never thought it would come to a trial in a Sheriff Court. Maybe I should have pleaded guilty, because in so many ways, I was.

And after all, the Jo Ricks joke was entirely mine.

"Ah, Flo," I told her, patting her headstone. "My dear old Nan. You desperate, lonely, nasty, vicious old bitch."

I stood up, peeling my t-shirt away from the granite. I probably had her name branded mirror-fashion into my back, but she couldn't drag me back, she couldn't make me stick to her forever. I hefted my pack and its deadly contents, and I walked away from her grave down the cinder path, and I didn't look back once.

Gillian Philip

24

It seemed like a coincidence, but I think it was just a kind of final, poetic farewell: I had to step back into the roadside undergrowth to let a white BMW hurtle past on its way out of town. I caught a glimpse of its occupants: Lily, enraged, was screaming at her father as she drove, paying no attention to the road. He was in the passenger seat, leaning forward to prop his hand against the dashboard in an instinctive attempt to protect himself. Good luck with that, I thought; your arm might shatter just a little before the rest of you. I only caught a glimpse of Brodie's quietly livid expression; most of my focus was on Lily's beautiful, furious face.

Good. I hoped their relationship was destroyed by this. I hoped she'd crash and kill... Brodie. Just Brodie. Not herself. She'd let me down but I didn't hate her.

When the car had passed and the grass on the roadside had stopped quivering and even the echo of the engine's roar had faded, I stepped out of the bushes and trudged the last half mile home. I took the quick route over the fence and climbed the steps to the back door.

The house was surprisingly cold for a summer night, with that particular chill houses get when they're empty and unloved. The cat flap vibrated in its frame as I shut the door, and I expected Marv to come shooting from the shadows into my arms, but he didn't. No small furry shape crept out of the darkness, though I could certainly smell the cat piss.

I dumped my backpack and walked on into the lounge. For some reason I didn't want to turn on the lights, but at last, my fingers shaking, I reached out and flipped the nearest switch.

"Marv?" I whispered.

"Marv?" I said more loudly.

I stood very still. The silence was so very loud. From the depths of it, I heard something else: a distant, feeble cry.

Marv always had a sissy meow, like a girl cat, but even so there was something wrong with it. I ducked down onto my hands and knees and crawled along the carpet, peering under the furniture. It was his eyes I saw first beneath Flo's old armchair, dilated to glowing orbs of pain and terror.

I stood up sharply, and hefted the chair aside, dumping it so hard the ornaments around the room rattled. There where the chair had been lay Marvin, not curled up but stretched and twitching. There was so much blood on his fur I didn't know where the wounds were.

I probably shouldn't lift him but I couldn't help myself. I gathered him into my arms, holding him close to my chest, getting dark cat-blood all over myself. He began to purr fiercely and snuggled his nose into my neck.

"Not you," I said, and I kept saying it over and over. "Keep breathing. Don't stop. Don't stop. *Don't stop.*"

*

I hammered and hammered on Crow's back door with one fist, my other arm still nestling Marv against me, wrapped in the softest towel I could grab. My heart was thrashing so hard I was dizzy, and any minute now I was going to throw up. I didn't even bother to hope that Crow's parents weren't home, but of course they weren't anyway. It was a bleary Crow who opened the door himself, in World of Warcraft pyjamas that were too small for him, his eyes widening as they took in the state of Marv.

"My phone's dead," I said. "Give me your phone. *Give me your phone.*"

When he offered it, I snatched it without so much as a thank you. I was nearly weeping as I waited for the ancient thing to load the Google page of vets and their contact details.

"What happened," said Crow, flattening his spiky hair with both hands. "What happened."

"I don't know," I snapped.

"Was it the big fox."

The big fox. The fox. The damn fox. I muttered the first phone number to myself, over and over, as I tapped it into the dial pad.

I heard an electronic voice tell me the surgery opening hours, and I hated that robot more than I hated Brodie Cumnock. Then I heard her say, "Please hold for emergencies," and the call clicked over to a new line, and a different phone begin to ring. I thought of the vet turning over in bed, reaching out slowly to answer the emergency call. *Wake up,* I thought at him. *Wake up, you lazy bastard.*

He was a her. She answered after three rings—was that really all?—and I gabbled something about Marv, and foxes, and not having a car. I have no idea what I said, but I think it involved cursing. She was surprisingly tolerant, because all she did was ask in a warmly professional tone for my address. I babbled it out, only just remembering the postcode in time, and I hung up before she did.

"That fox had a go at Mrs Slater's cat last week." Crow shrugged. "That one fights back though."

I gazed down at Marv. I couldn't decide if he'd fought back or not. I couldn't imagine he had, but I don't suppose it would have helped if he had. Marv was as crap at fighting as he was at finding the litter box.

"The fox," I repeated at last.

"Yeah, it's been at the bins. Doesn't scare easy. It lives in the woods just up the road there. I've seen it there." Crow shrugged. "I've seen its—"

"Please," I said. "Please come over and wait for the vet with me."

*

Bless the little bugger, he did. And he didn't leave afterwards, either. When I got back from the vet's at three in the morning—walking the whole way because I didn't want her to drive me back, not when she had Marv to look after—Crow was unconscious on my sofa, snoring. He'd pulled Flo's housecoat out of my backpack and tucked it round himself. Bits of shotgun lay abandoned on the carpet. My phone had recharged, so I unplugged it and shoved it into my pocket. I paused and looked at the shotgun pieces again.

I crouched to pick them up. I slotted in the barrels, and re-attached the forestock, snapping it gently into place. I glanced at the box of cartridges.

I should have been so tired but I wasn't, not any more. I felt as if I'd never sleep again. My brain fairly buzzed and my nerves jangled with hatred. Crow hadn't bothered to close the curtains; the sky was already tinged with bleached denim blue at the horizon. It hadn't been dark at all. There hadn't been a night. Why would I sleep?

I broke the shotgun, and took it for a walk.

*

The summer small hours seem to go on for ever. That dawn, I walked and I walked. I walked past my neighbours' houses and between their cars and out onto the road, and I didn't even think to key any bodywork. I walked through the outskirts of Langburn and past the primary school and the kindergarten, a shotgun nestled in the crook of my arm. I walked past the speed delimit sign, which was peppered with shot from teenagers who had nothing better to aim at, and I walked till I came to the gate into the woods, and then I walked some more.

There was no Sid at my side this time, babbling non sequiturs and casual gossip. It was so very quiet in the woods, and so very dark and peaceful, and I knew how to hunt, I knew how to stalk. When I was alone, I did. Early-riser rabbits darted and fled ahead of me, but I didn't fire. I didn't want a rabbit. I'd had enough rabbits. I'd had enough altogether.

Despite the improved stalking conditions, I found I missed Sid.

No, I missed Lily, I missed *Lily*. Anyway, Sid let me down. *Nothing's going to happen to Marv on my watch.* Well, it did. Sid let Marv get hurt.

No. *I* let Marv get hurt, because I abandoned him. That was what happened when you left things that depended on you. I stopped thinking that. I *made* myself stop. I even stopped walking for a moment, and tore gouges in my scalp with my fingernails while I tried to make my head settle.

I breathed, in and out, and shut my eyes, and opened them again, and felt a little more centred.

I moved more quietly after that, and I hunted through the dusty dawn-twilight trees, and when I found the den, just where Crow said it would be, I sank silently into a crouch, downwind of it and sheltered by the forest. I lay down on my belly, and I wriggled myself into the forest litter behind a rotted, crawling trunk. It probably helped that I stank like an animal.

The colours were so soft, so green and grey and pearl, and still the sun hadn't risen. There was no missing the dog fox when he slunk into the small clearing; even in the muted dawn his pelt glowed like copper.

I sank the stock firmly into my shoulder, and eyed him along the barrels. A faint breath of wind brought his scent to my nostrils. He smelt worse than me: musk and fox-scent and rotted trash. At least I think he smelled worse than me. It wasn't like I could smell myself much any more.

He licked his jaws, hesitated, snuffed the still air. His whiskers twitched, but he lowered his head and looked longingly towards his den. His ears pricked and swivelled and he turned a little towards me, his rusty flank presented. He wasn't scrawny; why would he be? He was sleek and well-fed, his eyes bright and dark all at once. He opened his jaws and his teeth were white and sharp. His pink tongue lolled suspiciously. His ribcage expanded and contracted with his breath. I could make out his heart, beating through his hide and his copper fur.

I didn't have long to do this. The fox's legs were surprisingly long and elegant; he was big, and he'd be fast. A lot of foxes are scruffs and ragamuffins, but he was very beautiful.

I stroked the trigger, cold iron tingling on my fingertip.

The fox went very still, and his eyes met mine.

He didn't move. I didn't move. Even my finger didn't move.

He was looking right at me, but his ribs and his heart were still in my eye line. A tremor ran down his flank. I watched him and watched him, my finger still as death, until he tensed, and sprang into fluid red motion, and vanished into the forest.

*

I lay there for ages, the deep chill seeping into my bones though I didn't feel it. I sort of knew I was cold; I just didn't mind about it. I wished I'd had the callous guts to shoot the fox. I didn't know what had come over me and now I'd let Marv down.

Everybody let everybody down. I sank my forehead into the leaf litter and I didn't think about anything else until I felt my phone buzz in my pocket.

I thought about not looking. When I pulled it out and saw the vet's number, I thought about throwing the phone deep into the woods. But she'd promised me to update me first thing in the morning. I had to know. I might as well know. I pressed the message icon.

Marvin resting quietly, it said. Surgery this a.m. No puncture wounds, some broken bones/internal damage. Suspect probs car. Will let you know any change.

Nice vet. She'd promised to let me know how he was and she hadn't let me down.

No puncture
Internal damage
Suspect probs car
Suspect car
Suspect.
Car.

*

"Did you not find the fox."

I'd know that flat inflection anywhere. I broke the shotgun, rolled onto my side and blinked up at Crow. He was still in his gruesome pyjamas, but he'd put on his cheap trainers and a thin jacket. It wasn't that cold a morning, but it was the hour before dawn, and it was pretty much the countryside, and he was shivering.

"No," I lied. "I didn't find it."

"That's too bad," he said. "I think you should just come home now."

"I'm not the one who's getting hypothermia." I nodded at Crow's trembling hands, and he shoved them into his jacket pockets.

"I'm worried about you," he said. "I think you should come home."

I didn't know what to say. I looked at the broken shotgun and ran my thumb across the shining brass caps of the two cartridges. I took one of them between my fingernails and twisted it in its barrel.

"Crow," I said, "I think I can finally understand why I put up with you."

He shrugged his scrawny shoulders.

"Nah," he said, and grinned. "It's just that I know where the body's buried."

I twisted the cartridge in its barrel again, another full circle. Then I blew out a breath, and snapped the shotgun back together.

Because Crow wasn't joking. Crow did know, metaphorically speaking, where the corpse lay. And maybe because he'd finally managed to say it out loud, he found himself a question mark at last.

"Eddie. I'm cold. I'm going back to the house," he said. "Please will you come too?"

Gillian Philip

25

MY GOD WHAT HAVE I DONE (1)

So.

I'm walking through the dawn again, through another pale half-light, but this is a truly cold one. There's lacy frost on every leaf, on every blade of grass. My arm is wrapped around Lily, and our breath is misting on the air, and there's plumes of it because we're both laughing. I can't look at us from an outside perspective but I *know* we're a beautiful couple. We're a perfect couple.

"I have to get back," says Lily, still gasping through giggles. "I said I'd be home in time this morning to feed Ponty."

"Ponty," I say. "*Ponty*. Pontchartrain is the stupidest name for a horse *ever*."

And that sets her off again. "He was called that when Dad bought him!"

I like the fact that she's laughing so much. It makes me laugh too and it helps me not think about how bad I feel. I shouldn't have stormed out on Flo last night, but she shouldn't have said what she did about Lily. She only said it because she was so angry and desperate and she didn't want me to go out again, but she went too far, yet again. And I was so exasperated with her clinging possessiveness and her sheer vicious rudeness, I simply walked out.

I know as I walk back towards the house that I've hurt Flo's feelings badly, but I'm not sorry. I'm so not-sorry, I barely regret staying out all night. Lily and I sat and drank (not much) and talked (a lot) at Aoife Connor's party, which as far as Brodie Cumnock knew was another all-night study session for Lily's girl pals from Dunstane College. One of Lily's girl pals even gave her a cover story and a forged note from the housemistress. How could we not take such a rare and beautiful opportunity?

I wasn't surprised when Flo called a few hours later. She always did go too far, and she always got tearily remorseful afterwards. But I'd gone to get more drinks for me and Lily, and I'd run into Mackenzie and we were having a laugh. It was Lily who answered the phone. She was grinning at me when I finally got back to her.

"That was Flo," she said, rolling her eyes. She was smiling very hard indeed.

"Oh bloody hell, Lily. Should I call her back?"

"Nah, she's okay. She's calmed down."

"Sure?"

"I'm positive. Relax, Eddie. You know your nan." There were high red spots on Lily's cheeks, like there always were when she was excited, or when she'd been arguing. But it was a party, and she'd been drinking. Of course she looked flushed and high.

"Yeah." So I sat down at Lily's side, and grabbed her hair and pulled her in for a kiss. I didn't even take my phone back straight away. "Better let her stew, anyway. Serve her right. She's really calmed down?"

"Course. I knew she would. She'll be all sorry when you get back. She'll bake you cookies."

Lily had started giggling, and I did too, and I admit I put Flo right out of my mind, then. I was having much too good a time.

So anyway.

I barely think about Flo till we're on our way home.

We pause at the end of my street and Lily gazes up at me, smiling. There's dew clinging to her hair.

"I wish I could walk you home," I say.

"Are you kidding? He'd murder you. Flo would murder me!" She's giggling again with the breathless daring of our all-night escapade.

"All the same," I say. "Will you be okay?"

I know fine she'll be okay. I'm just looking for an excuse to spend longer with her. I'm reluctant to face a tearful Flo; I'd rather stay right here. My breath smokes and clouds. The cold is harsh on my lips.

Lily isn't.

There's a stunted skinny figure in the corner of my eye, emerging from the house next to mine. He's wearing nothing but trainers and World of Warcraft pyjamas that fit properly. He starts to walk faster and wave as he sees me.

"Crow." I roll my eyes.

"I better go," says Lily, before she kisses me again. She turns her head as she walks away, and smiles at me, that come-hither closed-lipped smile that's all the more seductive because she doesn't know she's doing it.

I sigh with adoration and repressed lust. But I can't watch her walk away because Crow's running now, he's running in that gangly urgent way that means he's got something to tell me.

"Eddie," he pants. "Eddie, I think your nan's poorly."

Poorly means a very particular thing in Crow's world. Crow's dad is often poorly, when he's around. Crow jogs to a standstill, his message delivered, and smiles in satisfaction at a job well done.

"How is she poorly?" I ask, confounded.

"I was up early and I went to go and use your Xbox and I went to knock on your door and I heard your nan coming in a hurry and I shouted and she told me to feck off and then I heard her fall over on the stairs and she didn't say nothing else."

Then he turns and runs back, still gangly, less urgent. I hesitate for only a moment before I run after him, overtaking easily, my breathing suddenly loud in my ears in the frosty quiet morning.

He goes to follow me into the house as I slot in the key and open the door. I turn on my heel.

"Go home, Crow. I'll look after her."

He gives me a resentful look, but he does what he's told and goes home. I watch him clamber over the low fence between our houses and then I slam the door shut.

Flo isn't lying on the stairs. I frown. "Flo," I call. "Nan!"

She's not in the kitchen, where Jesus Gerard Butler points disapprovingly at me. She's not in the lounge. Marv stretches and claws the sofa, looking at me quizzically, but I don't stop to stroke him. Flo must have got herself back upstairs and gone back to sleep. She can't have hurt herself badly. I hope she hasn't.

"Flo!" I run up the stairs.

Her bedroom door's shut and there's no answer when I knock, so I burst in.

Flo's lying on the bed on her back. I can't hear her breathing, and her eyes are slitted. I don't know if she can see me. I walk over to her, not as fast as I'd have expected, and I put my fingers to her throat. I don't think I can feel a pulse. I'm not sure.

The feeling that squeezes my heart is a funny one. It's not relief. I don't know what it is. Anyway, it's overtaken by a surge of pity. That in turn subsides.

The laptop sits on the dressing table as it always does; the lid's open but the screen's gone to its big-eyed kitten screensaver. I'm still looking around, in a daze, and I blink at Flo's little side table. On it stand a half-empty bottle of Xanax and an empty bottle of gin. The labels are turned towards me so I can quickly see what they are.

There's a sliver of drool at the corner of Flo's mouth, discoloured by a hint of vomit. I put my finger against her throat again. There might be something there, something very faint, but it's the last of her. Something gurgles in her gullet. As I watch, it catches and chokes and her body goes into a little spasm, and a little vomit splashes on the wall beside her. Then she goes still again. She stays still.

I think she's stopped. I don't know what to do. My brain doesn't work.

My phone's in my hand. I reach out to take hold of the gin bottle, then draw it back and clench my fist.

I put my phone back in my pocket.

I tuck her duvet cosily round her, change my mind and loosen it again. I back slowly away as her glazed, half-lidded eyeballs watch me.

I close the bedroom door. I walk downstairs and out of the front door and out of the gate.

I walk faster. And faster. I keep going, heading for the bus stop, as Crow stands at his front window and watches me go.

26

Please will you come home too? Crow had asked, with that question mark and everything.

I didn't go with him. I didn't have to, after all. I wasn't duty-bound to feed or stroke or cosset or devote my life to another living soul. I had nothing to do but walk, and I liked walking now. I could imagine walking forever. I hitched the crooked shotgun over my arm and I walked out of the woods and I kept on going. Distantly there were echoing intermittent gunshots on the still air; the sound of the country. I wasn't the only hunter out in the early morning. If somebody saw me, I could pretend to be one of them, out for rabbits and foxes.

Why I should have to pretend anything else, I couldn't quite think.

Walking helps you think, though, so I tried to remember what had *gone through my head* when I closed my phone and walked out of that house six months ago. I'm sure Flo was dead. I think she was dead. I came in time for the absolute final moments. She couldn't have been saved.

But it was a bit of a blur. I remember fragments of thought: *If she wants it that much* and *I'll be tied to her till I'm fifty years old* and *Lily Lily Lily* were all in there somewhere.

I walked. I stopped, and eased the aching arm that held the shotgun, and then I gripped it more securely and walked again.

She was dead already, even if there was a last breath left in her. I didn't kill her. She killed herself. Maybe not on purpose, but effectively she'd done it to herself.

And Lily had done it to her too. Because Lily lied to me.

I knew straight away, but way too late, that she'd lied. I could almost have reconstructed the whole phone call. Flo, furious, screeching. Lily, exasperated and insolent, not listening to Flo's demands but to the voice of experience, the one that whispered *attention seeker, drama queen, emotional blackmailer*.

Flo hadn't called to tell Lily she was fine, not at all. She'd called to demand my return. She'd made her threats and shouted her ultimatum and Lily had hung up on her. And then Lily had lied to me. She as much as admitted it, later, when I asked her.

I didn't know she was serious, Eddie. I'm sorry, so sorry. And Lily had cried so hard, and her tears were so obviously real, I couldn't do anything but forgive her.

At least, I thought I had.

As I walked and walked that summer morning, I didn't know where I was going, or I didn't think I knew. I didn't know till I was there. I didn't know till I was standing at the paddock fence staring at the beautiful shining sprawling house that Brodie Cumnock built.

How did I get here? I thought, and I had to halt my train of thought right there. Otherwise it would run on and on and it would never stop.

Pontchartrain of the Stupid Name wasn't in the paddock. The whole place looked deserted: stables, yard, professionally landscaped garden. I gazed stupidly from one end of the place to the other.

He destroyed my life, I thought. *He's said I'll never see Lily again.*

Did I care? Lily lied to me. Lily lied to me in the worst way possible. She didn't even just lie by omission. She *lied.*

For God's sake, Lily as good as killed my own nan. And she might have made me an accessory, but I would never know. There was no way of knowing, now, if Flo had really been dead. *For God's sake. For God's sake.*

No nan no job no money no future no Lily no life.

Brodie's destroyed me. Lily too. They might as well have killed me.

That night, Flo must have expected me to rush home. She'd never have believed I'd stay out all night, not when we'd had a fight. She'd thought Lily would warn me. Would pass on the message. Those high red spots on Lily's cheeks, the way she was almost throwing the phone down as I returned.

How long did Flo put off taking the gin-and-Xanax cocktail after she phoned Lily to threaten it? How carefully did she calculate it? She'd had a previous experience; she knew what she was doing. She wanted me to find her again, she wanted me to arrive in time.

Well, maybe I did. I was never going to know.

And the worst thought of all: *I didn't want to know.* Not then. I walked out of her room and out of the house and down the road, and I did everything I could to *not-know*.

When Crow arrived in the early winter morning to borrow the Xbox, did she think it was finally me? Did she stagger downstairs in the befuddled notion that I'd rap on my own door? She must have thanked her vague happy-clappy God that I was back. Maybe by that time she was getting scared; scared and sleepy. But she'd timed her call right, by the skin of her teeth, and she must have been swamped with relief, anticipating another weepy reconciliation, another renewal of my vows.

That, she didn't get.

But it was summer now. It was all in the past, it was all in the winter past. The sky was more than tinged with dawn now; it was an arc of silvery grey. It was the hour just before dawn, the quietest hour, but it wasn't the darkest hour, whatever they say. It wasn't dark at all; the sky was melting from grey to palest blue even though the sun hadn't risen.

Nothing to do about it, nothing to fix any more. It was all in the past.

But somebody wasn't. Somebody wasn't, not yet, and he'd never let me down.

Marvin wasn't in the past.

27

MY GOD WHAT HAVE I DONE (2)

So I don't run. I do what I've found I like doing; I walk. I walk all around the perimeter of Brodie's house. Well, I skulk. I stalk and creep as if I'm hunting a fox. I walk around the edge of a field to the border of his land, where rough grass gives way to fences and shrubs and neat flowerbeds enclosed in rabbit-wire. The rabbits have got in anyway; some plants are bitten down to stalks. What do I care? Rabbit-damage isn't a priority in my life any more. My heart is beating so hard it's making me light-headed as I slink towards the sprawling house and its immaculate outbuildings.

The double garage is on the far side of a spotlessly-clean paved yard; somebody has already opened its electric doors. Of course the Cumnocks are early risers, with the horse and the land and the profitable but demanding business. Maybe not as early as vets with emergency cases, but earlier than your average Joe.

Nobody is in sight, so I duck and dart inside. The Beamer is the car nearest to me and it's been parked bonnet-first, so it's easy enough to walk round to the front of it without being seen.

I crouch. Even now, I don't want to find anything. But I do anyway.

The nose of the thing is sleek and aerodynamic, but still: stuck to the nearside corner there are tufts of black fur, a long streak of blood. I pick at the fluff, pulling it gently away as if I'll be hurting Marv if I tug too hard. It sticks to my fingers and I rub them together.

You'd think she'd have cleaned it off, really.

Except she hasn't cleaned it off because she hasn't even noticed. Lily hasn't *even noticed*. I remember the rush of speed, the bend and shiver of the roadside weeds, the roar of the car's engine in my ears.

She didn't even notice.

What's it like living inside Lily's head, I wonder? Is it suffocating in there, with no windows to the outside world?

I edge to the door of the garage, almost forgetting the shotgun is in my arms; it's a dead weight, is all. Lily's silhouette is visible at the kitchen window. She isn't sitting down, but chewing on a cereal bar as she goes about her morning business, her hair pulled back into a long stylish bunch. She isn't looking out of the window, and her father is nowhere in sight, so I sneak out of the garage and half-run to the stables round the corner.

Inside, I can hear Pontchartrain as he shifts and shakes his mane and scrapes the cobbled floor with an impatient hoof. He's in a stall, one of three in a row. (Brodie's planning for three horses. Jesus.) The haynet in the corner holds a few straggly shreds; Lily hasn't fed him yet. I step very cautiously into the dusty shade and duck into the stall beside Pontchartrain's. Along its wall are stored sacks of feed and chemical fertiliser; the smell is strong enough to sting my nostrils but not unpleasant. There's a wooden partition between me and the horse that comes up to my chest, and iron bars above that.

She loves him like I love Marvin.

I rest the shotgun through the bars. Pontchartrain snorts in nervous annoyance, and rolls his eyes back to glare at me, showing the whites. His head comes up and his neck arches and he looks suddenly spooked.

Pontchartrain for Marvin.

He deserves it if only for his stupid, stupid name.

Ponty for Marv.

Footsteps sound on the paving outside, and I duck back. I can feel Lily in the atmosphere before she even speaks.

"Morning, Ponty!" She sounds wide awake and happy as she bustles around with haynets and buckets; a boxful of grooming brushes clatters as she drops it to the ground. A shovel scrapes as she clears the shit. Why can't she feel *me* in the atmosphere?

I ease up, my back against the partition, and turn carefully sideways. My fingers are sweating, so I clasp the shotgun tighter. I peer over the wood and between the bars.

She won't know what hit her. The voice in my head is an alien one, except that it's mine.

I should be horrified, but the trouble is, I don't really feel anything any more, except a vague desire for things to stop. Me, Lily, Brodie, whatever. *Just stop.*

Anyway. It's not like she'll be able to smell you, between the horse and the fertiliser. All you have to do is wait for a clear line.

Oh the clamour of voices. They seem to have been yelling at me for months, so at least it's nice to have them saying something different. I find myself wondering if their thoughts would fit in 280 characters.

Lily is crooning to Ponty the whole time. Shushing him like a baby, calming him down as he grows restless. I recognise the tone; it's the one she sometimes uses to me. And she loves that horse, doesn't she?

She runs her hand down his foreleg, picks up his hoof and scrapes at it with something metal. He bends his huge head to nuzzle her, and blows at her silky hair. I start to ease the shotgun into firing mode. I'll just have to keep the click very quiet.

There. You can get an angle from here and she won't even see you unless she looks up. Yes, that one was well within the character limit. Well played, Voice.

"Good boy," Lily's saying. "Good lad." Her palm slaps his neck affectionately. I want to smoke. So, so much. How can I hold the gun steady if I can't have a smoke? But I can't light a cigarette, she'll smell it.

"Paddock time, baby. Good boy."

She swings open the stall door and I watch her lead him out, her fingers idly scratching his muzzle. He paces obediently at her side, hooves ringing loud on the hard surface, but his eye swivels back suspiciously towards me. Lily soothes him again and leads him on out into the morning sunlight.

Click Bait

I was never going to do it.

Hunter? Caveman? I can't even shoot a damn horse, much less the girl I used to love.

It's the fox all over again. Worse than the fox, because the fox didn't kill my cat. I slide back down the partition and sit against it, cradling the crooked shotgun like my firstborn baby, and feel something hot and wet on my cheeks. I wipe it off.

When my legs let me, I stagger up and lurch into the yard. I stop and heave a couple of breaths to ease the dizziness and to stop me throwing up. Then I sidle round the stable wall and prop myself at the corner, watching the house.

While I still stand there, peering round the corner of the stable block and wondering *what the hell is going through my head*, Brodie emerges from the back door and strides across the yard.

There isn't any urgency about Brodie Cumnock's movements. He's all relaxed confidence and easy wealth. He has a place in the world and he's sure of what it is. He pauses and examines the shotgun in his hands, then breaks it, rummages in his pocket and slots in two new cartridges. He raises his head, gazes around, and strides away from me towards the wood.

Rabbits are eating his flowers; he's killed my whole life. And this is his priority. The rabbits.

Don't you walk away from me DON'T YOU WALK AWAY.

And then I know, I know what I'm going to do. It's so obvious.

*

I snap the shotgun closed and ready, the echo of it thunderous on the still morning air. I haul myself over the yard fence and land on the wet grass with a thump. I jam the gunstock into my shoulder and sprint towards Brodie, watching him bob and jerk in my sights.

I stumble a bit, because aiming the gun is awkward, but I keep running, my jaws clenched. In anything other than my narrow intent vision, Brodie isn't bobbing and jerking. He has turned to face me and he's absolutely still, watching me with shock. But he doesn't panic, he doesn't even yelp. He snaps his own gun together and raises it and targets me, narrowing his eyes.

I run faster. I'm getting closer, and he isn't moving, and he isn't shooting. He just watches me along the double barrels of his silver-chased shotgun, and breathes gently: I see his chest rise and fall as his eye and his aim stay level on me. I'm growling at a high fevered pitch and I'm still running and I'm starting to wave the shotgun now and *doesn't he see the bloody thing?*

I stagger. I stop. I come to a halt three metres away from him, gasping and shaking.

He lowers his gun slightly. I keep mine aimed at his chest.

He lets his gun rest. He smiles at me, rather sadly.

"I'm not going to shoot you, Eddie."

I can't speak; I can hardly get air into my lungs. I shake the gun again, aggressive and pathetic at the same time.

"Put it down, Doolan. You're being ridiculous."

I'm starting to be able to breathe properly, and that means I begin to tremble. I clench my jaws and refuse to cry.

"I told you. I'm sorry about what's happened to you, Eddie; I actually am. I surprise myself sometimes."

I want him to surprise himself even more. I flick off the safety on my gun, and settle the stock tighter into my shoulder. I aim at his head. *I dare you. I double dare you.*

He tenses for a moment; just an instant. The he looks away. He actually looks towards the wood.

"I can just about shoot a rabbit, Eddie, but if you remember, I couldn't even shoot a deer. I'm not going to indulge you. Just live with it, Eddie. Live with your own bloody actions; nobody else cares."

I breathe out, my head light from a lungful of air held too long. I shake my head frantically.

"All right." He breaks his gun, balances it in his hands for a moment, then turns and begins walking away again. "Live with it or don't, but I'm not helping you. Not with a job, and not with a faceful of shot. Get off my property."

I watch his retreating back. I watch him hook the gun over his elbow and climb the stile. I watch him saunter into the woods and disappear among the trees and the shadows, and maybe a minute and a half later I hear the echoing crack of a gunshot.

A rabbit.

I break the shotgun in my arms. I'm less threat than a rabbit; I'm worth less than a rabbit. I walk back a few paces, then turn and shamble away. I can't go back through the yard; Lily will see me from the paddock. The utter, swamping disgrace is bad enough, but she's not going to witness it. I take a wide arc through the field and join Brodie's drive much further down towards the Langburn road.

I'm scared. So scared I can hardly focus. On top of everything else, I'm a coward. Oh, great.

I walk. Again.

Can I go down to the Dot Cumming Memorial Park and maybe find Drew and shoot him? Or Mackenzie Clark? Could I maybe shoot a bunch of strangers and go out in style? You'd be surprised how tempting it is. I'm already the bad guy; at least I'll be a bad guy with a decent bit of infamy: the bad guy who finally took control of his own life and that of several others. No, just Drew. Drew and Mackenzie and me, in a Mexican stand-off with just one gun.

I'm toying with myself to kill time, that's the truth. I know fine I can't shoot anybody. Not even Drew. *Especially* not Drew, funny as it seems. If I can't kill Lily—who I used to love, who was everything to me—there's no way I can kill Drew.

It's a beautiful morning, almost too beautiful to stand. There's a slight mist in the hollows, and sunlight is caught in it, making it luminous. On the clear air I can smell the porridgy scent of the distillery. Some people can't stand it but I've always liked that smell. It fills the Burnside Cemetery as I push open the gates and trudge up the driveway.

Pale granite headstones gleam in the morning light, all clean and shiny and new. Dewy silver spiderwebs hang on the bushes like yesterday's laundry. The pearly mist is slowly evaporating off the green grass, and threads of it still float in dips and ditches and a freshly-dug grave, but it isn't even a little bit creepy.

Joanna Ricks' grave is still heaped in flowers. Like she's barely dead. Like she's just under the surface, breathing softly, waiting for me. Opening her arms.

Click Bait

How could you do it to me, Eddie?

It isn't ever going to stop, I realise. From the moment I clicked *Post*, it was never going to end. I threw a lit cigarette into a dry forest, like an idiot, and when that kind of fire starts, it doesn't stop of its own accord. When did I start wanting to kill everyone? I can't remember, but that's exactly the thing, you *can't* kill everyone. And if I can't kill every last soul involved, then there's never going to be a firebreak.

And Lily: well, she lied to me about Flo's phone call, but I'm the one who chose to believe her. And it really was a choice. Everything I've done from day one has been my choice. Even believing Flo was dead: that was my choice.

"Yeah, sorry about that." I sit down on Flo's grave and pat the grass, then stroke it gently. She's right there, just a grass-blade's depth away, I can feel her.

I lean back on her headstone. "Bet you didn't think you'd see me back this soon."

She seems pleased. I think she's pleased. She never wanted to lose me, after all. The one thing, above all other things, that terrified her.

"Flo, I am in the deepest of deep shit," I tell her. "The police will be coming. I forgot an important date, but honestly, that's the least of it. Just don't be embarrassed when they turn up. It's got to stop somewhere."

I lock the shotgun into working order and prop its stock between my knees. I lean my forehead against its barrel and fumble experimentally with my fingertips for the trigger. It's actually bloody awkward. I move the barrels to my throat. Slightly easier. Chest? Worse. Back to throat. Sheesh. Everything has to be so bloody *difficult*.

Don't get me wrong, I don't actively *want* to stop. But nothing and nobody else will. Something has to.

I stretch clumsily down again for the trigger and a real live voice says:

"Eddie. Eddie."

It definitely isn't Flo.

I sigh. Can't help myself. I tilt my head back against the headstone again as Crow creeps nervously out of the pines and takes a few paces towards me. "What."

"Don't do that."

"Oh for Christ's sake, Crow, what are you doing here? Am I that predictable?"

"Yes."

"I wish you'd go away."

He shoves back his spiky hair. "No."

"Listen to me, you little scrote. I want you to understand. I've thought about it, okay? It's not a spur-of-the-moment thing." He really needs to leave now. I can feel my determination crumbling. "It's completely logical and I want you to piss off now." Especially since I might cry again, any time.

"What about Marv. What about me."

"What?"

"Marv and me. What about us."

"Well you'll both *live*." I hesitate, and my heart cracks a little. "Unless Marvin's dead already. But you'll be *okay*."

"I won't though. I won't be okay. I need you Eddie."

"You need my Xbox."

"No because you gave that to me already didn't you. I need you Eddie."

I'm so bloody exhausted. I lean my forehead against the barrels till they bite into the skin, till it hurts worse than the inside of my brain.

It's starting again. Somebody needs me and can't manage without me and *what would I do without you Eddie. You won't leave me, will you.*

"Eddie. Please don't, Eddie."

I have to look at him. I don't want to, but I have to. He's still in those ridiculous pyjamas and his thin jacket, and the cheap trainers are soaking from standing in the grass among the trees. He must have come straight here when he realised I wasn't going home. He must have known I'd come here eventually, and he's waited all that time. Poor little Crow.

I haven't felt anything very much since the necessary deadening crushed the endless sick feeling in my gut. I don't want to disturb that blanket of numbness but Crow's chin is trembling and his eyes are starting to brim. I scowl at him and rub my thumb against the cold metal of the barrel.

Which is when it *goes through my head:* it all started with a barrel, and it's going to end with a barrel. It's such a terrible, unfunny joke that I laugh. And right after that I start to cry.

Yes, it's starting again: I'm going to have a dependant. A soul-crushingly dependent dependant, somebody who always needs me there, somebody who refuses to let me go. I can't stand it and it can't be helped.

And maybe because my blood runs ice cold at the thought, my brain abruptly clears. And I realise I don't mind too much, and my soul doesn't feel all that crushed.

Crow is refusing to let me go. It's the nicest thing anyone's said to me in forever.

His hands are shaking, with either cold or fear, but he squats down and wraps his bony fingers over the stock and the barrel, and pulls the shotgun very, very gently away from me. I don't resist, because if I do, the thing might go off in the little bastard's hands.

He stands and looks at it for a minute, making a face; obviously it bothers him a lot more than the incredibly lethal high-tech arsenal he's built up in Call of Duty. He slouches up to the pines and disappears into them, and when he comes back he doesn't have the gun. He wipes his hands on his pyjama bottoms and coughs.

"The thing. The trouble. I fixed it anyway, Eddie. That's what I wanted to tell you. I fixed it for you. I fixed it all."

I stare at him, not understanding. I open my mouth to ask him what he's talking about.

And that's when I hear the sirens.

28

HOW DID I GET HERE (2)

Crow was always borrowing my stuff. Everybody in Langburn knew it. *Everybody*. The neighbours saw him stalking me, all the time. Even Drew Hunter had heard me bitch about him. Crow borrowed my Xbox so often, I actually gave it to him, just to get some peace.

He was always in my house and all. He thought he owned the place.

He thought he owned my laptop; why, he practically thought he had a right to my identity. No wonder he trolled politicians, journalists and bereaved mothers without a thought for the consequences. No wonder he thought it was acceptable to hijack my Facebook and post a stupid, tasteless joke.

Not everybody believed that. Aoife Connor didn't believe it for a moment, and I'm not convinced the police did, either. But they couldn't disprove it. They couldn't prove Crow was lying through his baby teeth, and nothing they could say to him would shift his position. Not even a giant family pack of Haribo. He'd had a sudden crisis of conscience and he'd decided to own up and that was that.

I yelled the house down when he told me what he'd done. I did not encourage this perjury, believe me. But even I couldn't shift him. When I told the police he was lying, he said *I* was lying, that I'd been lying all along to protect him. The Procurator Fiscal was not keen to take the little sod at his word, and the police even less so. But I could have told them. If they'd asked me, I could have told them that interviewing Crow was futile. He was a stubborn little scrote and once he'd made up his mind to get his way, the only thing to do was duck and protect your head.

And everybody knew it. Everybody knew Crow thought he owned both me, and everything I possessed.

As Martin Innes said, it wasn't worth pursuing any more and the police knew it. I hadn't killed anyone, not that they knew of. They couldn't prove Crow was lying, and Crow was not for turning, and Martin Innes was going to make hay with his claims in a courtroom.

I'd had my God-help-me-no-one-else-will summer, and the police must have decided that would have to do. The warrant for my arrest was withdrawn. Court proceedings were dropped. I didn't even have to go there to be told, wrongly, that I wasn't guilty. *No-Pro,* said Martin Innes, jargonning his head off as usual with a professional smile that didn't entirely say he liked me.

Crow was in a *lot* of trouble. The police and social services were all over him—and his pointless parents, so there was that—but all the Procurator Fiscal could do in the end was shrug his black-robed shoulders and roll his eyes. There wasn't much public interest in prosecuting a lying ten-year-old toerag who probably didn't know good taste and sensitivity from a hole in the ground.

In a completely just world, of course, I'd still have had questions to answer. Crow wasn't the one who'd turned up at someone's remote country home first thing in the morning, looking crazy enough to make Brodie call the cops.

But Brodie didn't tell them about my gun.

I don't know why. He told them nothing about me threatening him (but then, I hadn't, really). He said nothing about me trying to provoke him into shooting me (it hadn't worked, after all). He called the police and told them there was an unbalanced ex-employee on his property, one who had just jumped bail, and no, he didn't know where I had gone but my recently-dead grandmother was in Burnside Cemetery if that was likely to be of any help, and by the way he was seriously concerned for my mental health.

And the funny thing is, I think he was telling the truth. I haven't seen Lily since; but then neither of us has tried. If Brodie knew I'd had my sights on the back of his daughter's skull for a few demented seconds, he might have acted differently, but he didn't know that. And he never will. I'll never tell a living soul. I'm too ashamed. I'm too sane again.

So Sid crept up to the cemetery one night and retrieved the shotgun and put it back in her father's gun safe, and I don't think she's dared touch it since. Which is how it should be, there being actual gun laws in this country.

That's fine by me. I don't feel like hunting anyway, not ever again. I'm remorseful about pretty much everything in the world ever.

I'd feel a lot worse if Crow had been slung in jail, but I'm not surprised they didn't charge him. He's a lot younger than me, and plainly an idiot of epic proportions. The police gave him a bollocking such as even he had never experienced, but it was all one to Crow. He shrugged it off. He continues to whine a bit, almost dutifully, about the attention from social services, but it's not like his parents give a toss. I think secretly he enjoys the attention.

And he has me tied by invisible string to his little finger, for ever.

I don't feel too bad for Crow, and I don't even have space to feel guilty about him taking the rap, because I'm guilted-out. Anyway, what's to be guilty about where Crow's concerned?

If 'life' is where you get to from where you started, that boy is winning at life.

29

"I got flowers for Flo."

Sid doesn't ring the bell; she never does these days. She just walks in, shuts the door and lays a cellophaned bouquet on my coffee table. It's got a 'reduced' sticker on it.

I don't get up. I sit on the sofa and scratch Marv's head, in the spot between the ears where he likes it best. He half-closes his eyes, and kneads my lap in bliss. He's uglier than ever, with those shaved patches on his fur and his torn ear, and I realise he's just peed on me again.

"I love you," I tell him, picking him up to kiss his nose. He begins to lick my chin, thoroughly. "I love you so much I'm not even going to shove you out the cat flap for that."

"Aw, thanks," says Sid with a simper. I glower at her.

The scrawny figure who's lying on the carpet, controller in his hands, gives a snorting dirty snigger, so I glare at him as well. Crow has in fact given me back my Xbox, in a manner of speaking, but there's nothing altruistic about that. Having the Xbox in his own house, he swiftly realised, removed his excuse for getting away from his occasional-parents or for intruding on my solitude. It's so much better now that it's back in my house, and he can pay it and me uninvited homage at all hours of the day and night. My lounge hasn't had a Crow-free twenty-four hours in months.

And funnily enough, I don't mind. Not remotely. Even if it's costing me a fortune in bacon.

I still don't see much of my other neighbours, and certainly not the ones at number 44. I like to think they're embarrassed. At least the new window's still intact.

Sid flicks back the lid of the returned laptop and peers at it suspiciously. She's taken it upon herself to police it. I still can't afford a new one, but the old machine works a bit faster since I deleted all my social media apps. "You haven't been on Twitter, have you?"

"No," I say truthfully. My whole online existence is reduced to email and an occasional Google search. I'm afraid of Twitter: it's forgotten me, bar an occasional 'Whatever Happened To' link to a news magazine, but I've grown to hate it the way you hate any addiction you'll always be trying to conquer. And I'm terribly afraid that one day I'll comment on something, or retweet something awful someone has said, and it'll snowball into what happened to me. I wouldn't wish that even on Brodie Cumnock. So there's no point in me being there just to tweet kitten photos. I'm not Flo.

"Good. Glad to hear it." Sid picks up Jesus Gerard Butler from his new place on the mantelpiece—I finally took the dresser to the dump—and waggles his superglued arm at me.

"Remember that Jesus Gerard loves you, but if he catches you on Twitter you'll be getting a hard slap and no supper."

"Yes, Miss Sidonie."

The arm comes off in her hand, so she swears and sets Jesus Gerard back in his place. "Did you phone Mrs Slater back?"

"Yeah," I say. "Don't fall over. She's giving me a job. Sort of on probation but it's a job."

"Why would I fall over?" Sid smirks. "I knew she was going to offer. That woman's got a heart of wet dough. She was feeling sorry for you even before Marv got hit. After that? She'd have been bringing you cookies in jail if she had to."

I kiss the cat's head again. I love my Marv.

From his prone position in front of the television, Crow cranes round to narrow his eyes at me. "So get a discount on the bacon and stop moaning about the price of it." He chucks the spare Xbox controller at me. "Can you come and play now."

I sigh. I hand Marv gently into Sid's arms, stretch my stiff back, and get down on my belly to begin my drive back to Los Santos. Crow has already crashed my Lamborghini twice in the levee, so the first thing my avatar does is nick it back off him.

"Oy," he says, and slashes me with a knife in my virtual face. "Some best friend you are."

Sid watches us punch each other to death. "Did you hear Lily Cumnock's going to college in *California*?"

I shake my head. I used to wonder if Lily felt bad when she realised what she did to Marv, but I stopped wondering a while ago. She paid the vet bill, apparently, but I forgot to thank her. Some days, I sort of can't remember who Lily is. I feel worse when I remember my intentions about Pontchartrain. But California: that'll be great. Lily will be fine. Lily will always be fine.

My mind has wandered a little and so has my onscreen presence, so Crow shoots me in the back.

Behind us, Marv chooses his own moment to jump down from Sid's arms and stretch, so she dusts her hands and picks up the cellophaned bouquet. "You're both boring. I'll take those flowers up to Flo."

"Not carnations, right?"

"Freesias and some kind of greenery stuff." She peers at them. "Half price in Tesco."

"Well," I say. "Tell Flo hi from me."

I don't feel like I want to go up to the cemetery again. Ever.

"Will do." Sid opens the lounge door. "Oh, I got some dinner. So I'm staying."

"You cooking?" I say, and add hastily, "No fecking badgers."

"Chicken korma," she says sulkily. "Tesco. Half price. Oy. Doolan."

I look up at her. Crow sniggers. I sigh. I stand up stiffly.

"Bye," I say.

I kiss her. I kiss her for a while. Nothing remotely awkward about it. I regret stopping.

"Miss me," she commands.

"Oh yeah. I will."

Crow mutters, "Embarrassing."

"About time," says Sid, and sniffs the flowers, and leaves.

And I wish I could tell you this is the end.

No, scratch that.

I can't even say I wish it was the end. There's only one ending that's the true one, and sometimes even that one's buried so shallow that you scratch the earth and it clambers out and you wish like hell you'd left it alone. Me and Crow and Sid and Marv—heaven's sake, even Mrs Slater—we didn't get an ending. We're left with something slightly right and slightly wrong and not quite finished.

I didn't get what I wanted. I didn't get it to stop: none of it and nobody.

And I'm glad.

*Other titles by **BLKDOG Publishing** which you may enjoy*

Citizen Survivor Tales
By Richard Denham

Citizen Survivor's Handbook
By Richard Denham & Steve Hart

The Paranormal Investigations of Mister Balls
By Richard Denham

I'm Not Being Racist, But…
By K. Lee

Blue Crayon
By Rowen Ingrid Parker

Dad Jokes
By K. Lee

Poems of a Broken Soul
By Iza Tirado

Fade
By Bethan White

Sacrosanct: Poems by Prison Survivors
By various authors

Lemonade
By Tom Ashton

A House Out of Time
By John Decarteret

Hour of the Jackals
By Emil Eugensen

Soft Hunger
By Lucrezia Brambillaschi

Robin Hood: The Legacy of a Folk Hero
By Robert White

Diary of a Vigilante
By Shaun Curtis

I Am This Girl: Tales of Youth
By Samantha Benjaminn

Arthur: Shadow of a God
By Richard Denham

Dark and Light Tales of Ripton Town
By John Decarteret

Mixed Rhythms and Shady Rhymes
By Teresa Fowler

Thin Blue Rhymes
By various authors

The Woe of Roanoke
By Mathew Horton

Weirder War Two
By Richard Denham & Michael Jecks

Broken
By Ivy Logan

Origins: The Legend of Ava
By Ivy Logan

A Storm of Magic
By Ashley Laino

Arthur: Shadow of a God
By Richard Denham

King Arthur has fascinated the Western world for over a thousand years and yet we still know nothing more about him now than we did then. Layer upon layer of heroics and exploits has been piled upon him to the point where history, legend and myth have become hopelessly entangled.

In recent years, there has been a sort of scholarly consensus that 'the once and future king' was clearly some sort of Romano-British warlord, heroically stemming the tide of wave after wave of Saxon invaders after the end of Roman rule. But surprisingly, and no matter how much we enjoy this narrative, there is actually next-to-nothing solid to support this theory except the wishful thinking of understandably bitter contemporaries. The sources and scholarship used to support the 'real Arthur' are as much tentative guesswork and pushing 'evidence' to the extreme to fit in with this version as anything involving magic swords, wizards and dragons. Even Archaeology remains silent. Arthur is, and always has been, the square peg that refuses to fit neatly into the historians round hole.

Arthur: Shadow of a God gives a fascinating overview of Britain's lost hero and casts a light over an often-overlooked and somewhat inconvenient truth; Arthur was almost certainly not a man at all, but a god. He is linked inextricably to the world of Celtic folklore and Druidic traditions. Whereas tyrants like Nero and Caligula were men who fancied themselves gods; is it not possible that Arthur was a god we have turned into a man? Perhaps then there is a truth here. Arthur, 'The King under the Mountain'; sleeping until his return will never return, after all, because he doesn't need to. Arthur the god never left in the first place and remains as popular today as he ever was. His legend echoes in stories, films and games that are every bit as imaginative and fanciful as that which the minds of talented bards such as Taliesin and Aneirin came up with when the mists of the 'dark ages' still swirled over Britain – and perhaps that is a good thing after all, most at home in the imaginations of children and adults alike – being the Arthur his believers want him to be.

Broken
(Book I of The Breach Chronicles)
By Ivy Logan

BROKEN BUT NOT LOST

The dark shadow cast by an ancient prophecy shatters an innocent family, but all that is broken is not lost and will rise again.

Half-blood sorceress, Talia, had a unique childhood. It might have been bereft of dolls but not of love. Instructed in combat skills and trained to escape detection, she was schooled to face an unknown menace. Yet, when her family's worst nightmare comes to pass, Talia finds her protected life spinning out of control. Everything she believes in, and everyone she loves, is cruelly snatched away. Talia is forced to flee the attentions of a mad king and denied her supernatural legacy.

She chooses the path of retribution, devoid of love and friendship, but learns that sometimes love is received even if not sought.

'Broken' is a tale about Talia's coming of age, reuniting with her family and seeking vengeance. Most of all it chronicles Talia's rise from the ashes and her journey into finding herself again.

Read Talia's epic saga of love, sacrifice, friendship, and discovering the hero within set against a background of time travel and supernatural forces.

**Weirder War Two
By Richard Denham & Michael Jecks**

Did a Warner Bros. cartoon prophesize the use of the atom bomb? Did the Allies really plan to use stink bombs on the enemy? Why did the Nazis make their own version of Titanic and why were polar bear photographs appearing throughout Europe?

The Second World War was the bloodiest of all wars. Mass armies of men trudged, flew or rode from battlefields as far away as North Africa to central Europe, from India to Burma, from the Philippines to the borders of Japan. It saw the first aircraft carrier sea battle, and the indiscriminate use of terror against civilian populations in ways not seen since the Thirty Years War. Nuclear and incendiary bombs erased entire cities. V weapons brought new horror from the skies: the V1 with their hideous grumbling engines, the V2 with sudden, unexpected death. People were systematically starved: in Britain food had to be rationed because of the stranglehold of U-Boats, while in Holland the

German blockage of food and fuel saw 30,000 die of starvation in the winter of 1944/5. It was a catastrophe for millions.

At a time of such enormous crisis, scientists sought ever more inventive weapons, or devices to help halt the war. Civilians were involved as never before, with women taking up new trades, proving themselves as capable as their male predecessors whether in the factories or the fields.

The stories in this book are of courage, of ingenuity, of hilarity in some cases, or of great sadness, but they are all thought-provoking - and rather weird. So whether you are interested in the last Polish cavalry charge, the Blackout Ripper, Dada, or Ghandi's attempt to stop the bloodshed, welcome to the Weirder War Two!

**A Storm of Magic
By Ashley Laino**

Being brought back from the dead is an impressive trick, even for magician Darien Burron. Now he must try and use his sleight of hand to swindle modern-day witch, Mirah, to sign her power away, or end up a tormented demon in the afterlife.

Meanwhile, sixteen-year-old Mirah is starting to lose control of her powers. After an incident at her aunt's Witchery store, Mirah is sent to a secret coven to learn to control her abilities. While away, Mirah meets up with a soft-spoken clairvoyant, a brazen storm witch, and the creator of dark magic itself. The young woman must learn to trust in herself before she loses herself entirely to the darkness that hunts her.

www.blkdogpublishing.com